A BAD BEGINNING

It was some time before Michael and Adele recovered from their disastrous first meeting in Turkey, but they grew closer as they worked together to try to solve a puzzle that threatened to turn into a tragedy. In spite of the idyllic setting, there was danger threatening them as unscrupulous opponents tried to carry out their plan to profit from a family's fears. Would the end of the holiday mean a new beginning?

Books by Sheila Holroyd
in the Linford Romance Library:

ALL FOR LOVE
THE FACE IN THE MIRROR
DISTANT LOVE
FLIGHT TO FREEDOM
FALSE ENCHANTMENT
RELUCTANT LOVE
GREEK ADVENTURE
IN SEARCH OF THE TRUTH
ON TRIAL
ISLAND INTRIGUE
PURITAN BRIDE
KEEP ME FROM HARM
FAITHFUL TO A DREAM

SHEILA HOLROYD

A BAD
BEGINNING

Complete and Unabridged

LINFORD
Leicester

First published in Great Britain in 2005

First Linford Edition
published 2006

British Library CIP Data

Holroyd, Sheila
    A bad beginning.—Large print ed.—
Linford romance library
    1. Romantic suspense novels
    2. Large type books
    I. Title
    823.9'14 [F]

    ISBN 1–84617–491–0

Published by
F. A. Thorpe (Publishing)
Anstey, Leicestershire

Set by Words & Graphics Ltd.
Anstey, Leicestershire
Printed and bound in Great Britain by
T. J. International Ltd., Padstow, Cornwall

This book is printed on acid-free paper

1

He was good-looking, with a straight nose and firm chin and thick black hair and when he stared down at his glass on the bar, Adele could see the long dark lashes against his tanned cheek. Helen nudged her.

'Don't just sit there gazing at him. Say something!'

Adele felt nervous, but there was a very attractive man sitting less than a yard away from her, obviously on his own. It was clearly her duty to try to make contact. She cleared her throat and turned towards him.

'Hasn't the weather been gorgeous today?' she said, and immediately felt very foolish.

Here in the Turkish resort of Kas, the weather seemed to be gorgeous every day, with endless blue skies reflected in the waters of the bay. However, it didn't seem to matter, as there was no response from the young man.

'He doesn't speak English,' she muttered to Helen.

'Try again. Perhaps he didn't hear you.'

At that moment, the hotel manager appeared behind the bar and said something to the stranger, who shook his head in response to the query and replied briefly in Turkish.

'I told you so,' Adele said, not troubling to lower her voice this time. 'He's Turkish.'

This time, the young man obviously heard and cast a quick look at her, but she did not see this and went on recklessly.

'He's probably just another carpet salesman looking for victims.'

The door opened and a fair-haired young man hurried in anxiously and went up to the dark stranger.

'How did you get on? Was there any news?' he asked.

'It was a waste of time. They couldn't

help,' the stranger replied in perfect English.

Adele sat still, a crimson tide of embarrassment colouring her face, while by her side Helen gasped and then started to giggle.

The stranger stood up and he and the newcomer made for the door, the fair-haired young man looking curiously at the two young women and smiling as Adele caught his eye.

After the door closed, Adele sighed gustily.

'Well, I certainly messed that up.'

'Don't worry,' Helen comforted her. 'I'm sure we'll find someone for you.'

'I don't want someone,' Adele began heatedly, but Helen was no longer listening, just biting her lip, her pansy-brown eyes suddenly serious.

'I'll just go and check if there are any messages on my phone,' she said, sliding from the bar stool. 'Are you coming?'

Adele shook her head.

'I'll stay here and have another

orange juice before I come up for a shower.'

When Helen had gone, Adele allowed herself a little grimace and an impatient sigh before she ordered her drink. She should have suspected something the day when Helen called to say that her husband, Roger, could not come on the holiday they had booked, so would Adele like to come with her instead. She should have asked why they didn't just postpone the holiday until they could both go, but as she was feeling ready for a break after working hard for several weeks she had readily accepted the chance of a holiday in Turkey with her friend.

Admittedly, she had been rather surprised that Roger was not there at the airport to see them off, but Helen had seemed in excellent spirits, chattering about the good times they would have. However, when they had reached the hotel and Adele had gazed out of the window and said that Helen must take some photographs of the view to show Roger when they got back, her friend had suddenly burst into tears.

'I'm not going back, not to Roger,' she sobbed. 'We haven't had a holiday for two years because we have been so busy setting up the shop and spending every penny we had on it. We were permanently tired and getting on each other's nerves, so I told Roger we both needed a rest and he finally agreed to come on this holiday. Then a week ago he suddenly said he couldn't come! Somebody had contacted him who might buy a lot of stuff and he'd arranged a meeting. I told him that the customer would understand if he had to wait a couple of weeks, but Roger insisted that the man couldn't meet him any other time. So I told him that he was obviously more interested in selling a few bits and pieces than he was in me, and that if he didn't come on this holiday I would leave him. And he refused to come!'

She had collapsed on her bed, sobbing while Adele murmured soothing reassurances. She remembered going to the opening of the shop. It stocked glass — beautiful vases and dishes and goblets — exquisite and very expensive creations, many of them designed by Roger himself. Adele had wondered at the time if there would be enough customers ready to pay the high prices and suspected that somebody willing to buy a large quantity would be very welcome.

'Don't be so upset. You'll feel differently after you've had a holiday, and Roger will miss you so much that he will be desperate to make it up with you,' she reassured Helen.

'Do you think so?' Helen said hopefully, fumbling for her handkerchief. 'He said I was stupid and he'd be glad when I'd gone because then he would get a bit of peace.'

Adele suppressed a smile.

'It sounds as if you had a good row. He'll feel like that for a couple of days and then he'll get lonely.'

'Perhaps I was wrong. Perhaps I

should have stayed with him.'

'Well, it's too late for that now. Don't worry. Let's enjoy the holiday.'

That had been three days ago and Kas had proved an easy place in which to enjoy oneself. It was a small, quiet resort in a setting of spectacular beauty. The bay's tranquil waters invited swimmers and hills rose behind the town, still covered with spring flowers.

The girls' hotel was on the waterfront, and they had spent a large part of the two previous days diving from rocky platforms into the sea, emerging to eat in one of the restaurants overlooking the bay. Sometimes they spent a pleasant hour or so wandering through the streets and gazing into the shops whose proprietors would often tempt them to come in to look at their wares more closely with the offer of a glass of hibiscus tea.

Helen was happy enough during the day, but as the evening sky began to darken, her mood would change and she would check her mobile phone, hoping to find that Roger had called and left a message. After the inevitable disappointment Adele would have to listen sympathetically while Helen ranged from anger towards her distant husband to guilty self-reproach for having abandoned him.

She was clearly regretting the ultimatum she had issued and Adele hoped that Roger would be waiting at the airport when they returned with a large bouquet of flowers so that the pair could have a passionate reconciliation. From what she knew of Roger, he was too proud to give in quickly.

She looked at her watch. Helen had had enough time to get over her inevitable disappointment and they could get ready to go out for their evening meal. Of course, Roger might have called. What would happen then? Would Helen insist on flying back to England immediately?

As Adele walked towards the door out of the bar, it opened and she found herself facing the tall, dark young man.

She hesitated, wondering whether to offer an apology, but compromised with a friendly smile, only to regret this as he simply ignored her and made for the bar. This time her cheeks were glowing with anger as she climbed the stairs. All right, she had been unintentionally rude, but she did not like being snubbed.

Helen was looking downcast. So Roger had not called, and Adele would have to try to cheer her up over dinner. This was getting a little boring. Maybe it was time to be a little less sympathetic.

As they sat in a restaurant eating freshly-caught sea bass she allowed Helen to complain about her unreasonable husband for ten minutes and then cut in.

'Has it occurred to you that Roger may be waiting for you to call him?'

Helen sat up indignantly.

'As if I would! I have my pride!'

'And so has Roger.'

Helen thought for a moment.

'But he was the one who wouldn't come on holiday!'

'Because he hoped to sell a lot of glass. Is the shop doing so well that you can afford to miss a chance like that?'

'We've survived so far.'

'Just survived? What does the future look like?'

Adele went on ruthlessly as Helen stayed silent.

'You knew you were taking a risk when you opened the shop, but it gave Roger independence and an opportunity to develop his own talents. If the shop has to close, he'll have to go back to working for somebody else, churning out the kind of thing they want, not what he wants to produce.'

'He's putting the shop before me!'

'And you are putting yourself and this holiday before him, before his one opportunity to fulfil his dreams.'

Slowly, Helen began to eat again, looking both thoughtful and resentful. Adele gave a little laugh.

'Don't be angry with me. I'm only

trying to give you another view of the situation. I seem to be offending everyone today. That man I accused of being a carpet salesman cut me dead.'

The distraction worked. Helen looked up with lively interest.

'He did? What a pity he heard what you said! He looked the right type for you.'

Adele couldn't quite understand why Helen, apparently on the point of breaking up her own marriage, was still convinced that every girl over twenty should have a husband. Every time she had been invited to their flat over the shop, Adele knew that Helen would have managed to find an eligible man to meet her, in spite of the fact that Adele constantly assured her friend that she was enjoying her career as a very junior accountant and could find her own partner if she ever got the urge to marry. But Helen persisted in viewing her as lonely and in need of a husband.

'Forget possible boyfriends,' Adele now said firmly. 'I've been looking at the guide book and there is an amphitheatre at the other end of town. We can walk there tomorrow.'

'I thought I might go and have another look at the jeweller's in the main street,' she said hurriedly.

'You can't afford jewellery, and you'll enjoy the walk,' Adele told her.

The second part of that statement had definitely been wrong, Adele thought grimly to herself the next day as she trudged resolutely along the dusty road, trying to ignore the burning heat of the Turkish sun. A cry of pain made her stop and look back. Helen was hobbling badly.

'I've got a blister!' she complained.

'Well, I told you those sandals weren't suitable for walking,' Adele said wearily.

Her friend lowered herself gingerly on to the parched grass by the side of the road.

'I didn't realise how far we would have to walk to see your old amphitheatre, and then it was just a few rows of rocks and some bits of wall.'

Adele sat down beside her, secretly glad of a chance to rest but wishing there was more shade.

'That amphitheatre is thousands of years old. What did you expect? Something like Windsor Castle?'

This was probably true, she admitted to herself. Helen was a very bright girl in some ways but ancient history meant nothing to her, and her eyes tended to glaze over if Adele tried to explain the long history of Turkey.

Helen sighed, rubbing her foot.

'Well, at least you enjoyed it and I can say I've done something cultural.'

'Now, let's get back to the hotel and out of this heat. It is definitely hotter today.' Adele stood up and held out her hand.

'Take my arm and see if that helps.'

In fact the town of Kas was quite near but their hotel was at the far end and Helen's limp grew worse until she was leaning heavily on Adele. They stopped and drew to one side when they heard a car behind them, but instead of passing them by it drew up.

'You look as if you need help. Can I give you a lift?'

The speaker was in his twenties, with a pleasant face beneath a tousled thatch of corn-coloured hair. Adele recognised him as the man who had come into the bar the night before, the friend of the dark-haired man.

'Yes, please!' Helen said at the same moment as Adele's cold, 'No, thank you.'

The stranger lifted his eyebrows and looked from one girl to the other.

'I'd love a lift,' Helen said firmly. 'Are you coming, Adele?'

Faced with the choice between a comfortable ride back to the hotel or being abandoned in the heat while her friend vanished with a complete stranger, Adele joined Helen in the back seat of the car.

'I know you are staying at the same hotel as I am, so it's no trouble,' the driver said as he restarted the car. 'My name is Tony Edwards, incidentally.'

'I'm Helen Perry and this is Adele Pearson. So you are on holiday here as well?'

'In a way. I'm with a friend, but we are not sure how long we shall be staying in Kas. We might be here for some time.'

'Aren't you lucky!' Helen said, who only an hour before had been telling Adele how pleased she would be to get back to some cool English rain. 'We came for a fortnight.'

The car drew up outside their hotel and Adele got out quickly, but Helen lingered, leaning forward to give the driver a brilliant smile.

'I'm so grateful to you for giving us a lift. I don't think I could have managed to walk all the way back.'

Tony Edwards blinked, obviously dazzled, and hurriedly got out to help Helen get out of the car.

'I hope we will see you again,' she said, and Adele blushed at this heavy hint and hurried Helen towards the hotel door.

As they approached, it swung open and the dark-haired young man appeared. He was eagerly greeted by his friend.

'Michael! I've just done my good deed for the day and rescued these two ladies.'

There was a flicker of recognition in the eyes of the newcomer as he surveyed Helen and Adele and he nodded slightly. Adele was suddenly aware of how hot and dusty she must look.

'This is Michael Brereton. We are staying here together,' Tony said.

He looked at his friend questioningly.

'Have you heard anything yet?'

Michael Brereton shook his head.

'They might telephone later. I've told the manager that we will be at the Mermaid for dinner if there is any news.'

'The Mermaid?' Helen interrupted chattily. 'We were thinking of going there for dinner tonight.'

Adele was too taken aback by this

untruth to say anything before Tony said, 'Really? Then you must let us take you there.'

Adele tried to smile at Tony and look daggers at Helen at the same time.

'I think you've made a mistake, Helen. We were just going to have a quiet snack tonight.'

'Then change your plans and come with us,' Tony urged, obviously warming to the idea. 'We'd like you to come, wouldn't we, Michael?'

Michael, clearly torn between politeness and reluctance, nodded wordlessly while scowling.

'That's settled then,' Helen said blithely. 'We'll see you in the bar at eight.'

Once in the cool shelter of their room, Adele turned on Helen reproachfully.

'Didn't your mother ever tell you not to talk to strange men, and certainly not to accept lifts from them?'

Helen gave a mischievous grin.

'I'm sure that if she did she also said

that I could accept a lift if the temperature was over eighty degrees, I had a bad blister, and the stranger was a very nice young man.'

'Would she say that you should go out to dinner with him as well, especially when his friend obviously wants nothing to do with us?'

Helen shrugged.

'I'm doing it for your sake. We are going to have dinner with two good-looking young men so that you will have a chance to make up for insulting one of them. Anyway, I'm bored with waiting for Roger to call me. I want to go out and have a good meal and forget him.'

Adele plumped down on her bed.

'Helen, you are married!'

'So what? I'm going as your chaperone. Now, what are we going to wear?'

Resigned to dinner at the Mermaid, Adele took particular care over her dress and make-up in an effort to compensate for the poor impression she had made on Michael Brereton so far.

When they made their way down to the bar, she knew that although she might not be as alluring as Helen, she did look her best in her blue top and skirt. Tony was obviously impressed, and even Michael gave them an appreciative look before he finished his low-voiced conversation with the manager.

As they stepped out of the hotel into the warm air, Adele looked up at the stars beginning to appear overhead. It was a beautiful end to the day. The stresses of work in England could be forgotten for a while and she resolved to enjoy the evening.

'Do you think you can walk to The Mermaid?' Tony asked Helen anxiously. 'I can go and get the car if you like.'

Helen tucked her hand through his arm.

'I feel fine. Let's walk.'

She and Tony walked ahead chatting amicably, while Michael and Adele followed them, silently. Adele glanced up at her companion. He was a very attractive man, in spite of his coldness.

What a pity they had got off to such a bad start! She owed it to herself to show him that she was really a very nice person. Perhaps they could make a fresh start and become friends over the meal.

2

Adele and Helen had passed the Mermaid on some of their walks through the town. The entrance was unassuming, but they were greeted pleasantly by a smiling waiter who led them through a door into the restaurant area where Adele stopped and stared. The restaurant was built into the top of a cliff and the candle-lit tables were situated on balconies so that they had stunning views over the harbour and the sea.

'Impressive, isn't it?' Tony said. 'And the food is good as well!'

The waiter showed them to a table and gave each of them a menu. Adele looked at it with happy expectation. Then, as she hesitated between steak and swordfish, she caught sight of the prices and her eyes widened in horror. This was obviously one of the most expensive restaurants in Kas! She had intended to offer to pay their share, but knew that she and Helen had not brought sufficient money with them to meet the Mermaid's prices!

She looked anxiously at Helen, but her friend and Tony had their heads bent over the menu and were busy deciding what to order.

'If you are not sure what to order, may I recommend the swordfish? I usually have it when I come here.'

Michael Brereton's manner was cold, but at least he had let her know that he was familiar with the Mermaid so that the prices were not a complete shock. Reassured, she ordered the fish and they agreed on an assortment of appetisers for the first course.

Helen and Tony were chatting freely as if they had known each other for years, but Adele and Michael sat in silence once the meal had been ordered. Was he still brooding on her unfortunate remark about a carpet salesman? Stealing a glance at him, she saw that his head was turned towards the sea but that he seemed unaware of the glitter of silver moonlight on the water. Instead he was frowning and looked completely unaware of his surroundings, as though he was brooding on some problem.

'Have you been to Kas before?' she asked him, more to gain his attention than anything else.

He turned towards her and blinked uncertainly, as though he had been so deep in his thoughts that he found it difficult to remember who she was.

'Kas?' he repeated, and then, with an obvious effort, made an attempt at conversation. 'Oh, I've been here many times. My father is an archaeologist and we used to spend our holidays in Turkey when he was excavating some site in the country. Kas was our favourite seaside place. My sister and I . . . '

He stopped abruptly and Adele waited for him to continue, but he had fallen silent. Just then, the appetisers arrived and they were taken up making their selection. Later Adele tried again.

'Your father was an archaeologist? So you must know something about the amphitheatre. I took Helen there today, but I'm afraid she didn't think much of it.'

'You are interested in archaeology?'

From his tone, Michael was obviously surprised, and Adele flashed him a look of dislike. How dare he be so patronising?

'I have read about the Greek and Roman antiquities in Turkey,' she said stiffly, but now she had his full attention.

'That's a start, but there is so much more. Have you seen the rock-cut tombs?'

She shook her head, and at that moment Tony cut in.

'Very few visitors to Kas know that they exist, Michael. Why don't you take Adele to see them? You could tell her everything about them.'

'That's a good idea,' Helen said

24

warmly. 'Then I wouldn't have to go with her.'

Adele and Michael looked at each other warily. Adele longed to learn more about these mysterious tombs but was not sure that she wanted to go with Michael. He, obviously, was searching for a polite way out of taking her sightseeing.

'I would be delighted to show you the antiquities of Kas,' he said with an obvious lack of sincerity. 'Unfortunately, I don't have much free time in the next few days.'

'What about tomorrow morning?' Tony said ruthlessly. 'We have nothing arranged for then. We could all go!'

Helen looked apprehensive.

'Look round more ruins? Ancient history and ruins bore me stiff!'

'I don't find them very thrilling either,' Tony told her with obvious relief. 'In that case, I'll show you round some of the more attractive bits of Kas while Michael and Adele inspect the antiquities.'

Neither Adele nor Michael could produce any good reasons why this should not be possible and they found themselves agreeing to the plan, though it was obvious they would be reluctant companions. Adele thought what a pity it was that he was such a stuffy pain in the neck when he was so good-looking!

The food was delicious and the wine was good. Almost in spite of herself, Adele began to relax and enjoy the evening. This was how she had hoped Turkey would be away from the noisy bars and restaurants of some of its resorts. And she was going to have a guided tour of the area's antiquities! Michael Brereton might not be the companion she would have chosen but at least he clearly knew something about the area and its history.

As the evening drew to a close, Adele excused herself and went to the ladies' room, and as she came out she became aware of the heavy scent of jasmine drifting through the night air from some nearby garden. She paused to enjoy the perfume, and at that moment she heard Tony Edwards' voice nearby.

'I'm sorry you're not enjoying yourself, Michael. Helen and Adele are pleasant girls and I thought dinner out with them might distract you.'

Michael Brereton replied.

'Nice girls? I thought it was very obvious that they wanted a free meal and that was why they put us in a position where we pretty well had to invite them to be our guests.'

'I don't think that is fair,' Tony disagreed, and then their voices moved away and the words became indistinguishable.

As quietly as possible, Adele made her way back to the table, her cheeks blazing with embarrassment and anger. The two men were busy paying the bill. Adele was silent as they walked back to the hotel and in the foyer Michael turned to Adele.

'Shall we meet here at ten tomorrow morning? That is, if you still want to see the tombs.'

He was giving her a last chance to

back out of the arrangement, but although she had not spoken since she had overheard the conversation, now she nodded wordlessly.

Helen chattered away as usual as they prepared for bed, reviewing the evening and commenting on the restaurant, but Adele said little in reply. Finally her friend plumped down on her bed and stared at her.

'What's wrong, Adele? You're not listening to me and you've hardly said a word for ages!'

'I'm tired, that's all.'

'Well, Michael wasn't very stimulating company for you, was he? Anyway, perhaps he'll be more likeable when he's talking about tombs. You don't have to see him again after that if you don't want to.'

'I probably won't, but what about you and Tony?'

Adele looked smug.

'Tony and I enjoy each other's company. I won't mind going out with him tomorrow.'

Adele sighed. She decided not to tell Helen what she had overheard. Why should that stupid man upset both of them?

Adele and Helen were a little later than usual getting down to breakfast and there was no sign of Tony or Michael on the shady terrace where they took their meals. Adele was quite prepared to find that a polite message of regret had been left with the young receptionist, but when she came down to the foyer at two minutes past ten, both Michael and Tony were waiting there.

'Helen will be down in five minutes, or perhaps ten,' she assured Tony.

'Then you two may as well go,' he said cheerfully.

'I thought we could go to the amphitheatre first. I can probably tell you a few things that the guide books don't mention,' Michael said politely, as they set off along the road which led round the harbour.

It only took five minutes to reach the

edge of the small town, and when they reached a clump of trees, Adele halted. Michael turned to her enquiringly.

'Before we go any farther, I've something to give you,' she said before pulling a white envelope out of her shoulder bag and handing it to him.

Looking puzzled, he opened it and took out several Turkish banknotes. Adele took a deep breath and started on her carefully-prepared speech.

'That is to pay for the meal Helen and I had last night. I think you will find there is enough there. We came with you because we thought it would be a pleasant evening, and we were not trying to get a free meal. Now I know you don't want to take me sightseeing, so you can leave me here. I'm quite capable of looking at things by myself.'

What she did not tell him was that the envelope contained a large part of her remaining spare money. She had not yet worked out how she would survive for the rest of the holiday but had decided during a restless night that this was the only way she could show Michael Brereton how wrong he had been about her and Helen. She would at least have the satisfaction of hearing him apologise, of seeing him look ashamed of himself, even if she had to live on bread and oranges for the next ten days.

Realisation had dawned in his dark eyes.

'You heard me talking to Tony!'

'Yes! And you were wrong about us.'

He looked at her for a long moment, his lips twitched, and then, instead of collapsing with embarrassment he threw back his head and roared with laughter. She waited, stiff with annoyance, until he had finished laughing and was smiling broadly at her.

'I think we are quits!'

'What do you mean?' she demanded.

'Aren't we equal now? You insulted me by assuming that I was waiting for a chance to sell you a carpet, and then I insulted you because I thought you two just wanted a meal at our expense.'

He pushed the notes back in the envelope and handed it back to her.

'Here, take it. We invited you to be our guests and I don't want it.'

She put her hands behind her back defiantly.

'No. I want to prove that you were wrong about us.'

'Clearly I was wrong. You wouldn't have offered me the money otherwise. We invited you to be our guests, and I am not going to take this.'

She had looked forward to regarding him with triumphant scorn when he accepted the money, and now she glared at him with furious frustration, as he grew more persuasive.

'Let's start again, Adele. If you won't take this money back, I shall insist on buying you a carpet, and how will you pack that?'

Suddenly she saw the comic side of the little scene and giggled. His expression relaxed and as he smiled down at her he seemed very different from the cold and distant figure of the previous evening. She took back the envelope and stuffed it into her bag with secret relief.

'Very well. Let's get on exploring.'

He proved to be very knowledgeable. Instead of the amphitheatre, he led her up the hill to some tombs which looked like miniature houses with stone benches where the dead could sleep away eternity.

She emerged from one with her face alight with interest, and was turning to ask Michael a question when she felt something hit her arm. As she swung round to see what was happening, a small stone struck Michael on the back and he turned as well. They saw an old peasant woman sitting under a tree. When she saw she had gained their attention, she put down the pebble she was holding and pointed up the path, smiling and nodding.

'We'd better do what she wants before she goes on to bigger rocks,' Michael murmured, and obediently they followed the path onwards and soon found themselves among more rock tombs.

'That old lady was obviously determined that we should see everything,' Adele commented, and they inspected the tombs happily for some time until she realised how hot the day had grown.

'I think it's time to get back to modern Kas and a long drink,' Michael announced, steering her towards the path that led back to town.

In five minutes, they were sitting under a cool awning and eagerly grasping glasses of orange juice. Adele drank gratefully and looked across at Michael. 'Thank you. I really enjoyed this morning.'

He gave her a mock salute as acknowledgement.

'So did I. A lot of girls claim to be interested in ancient history but that usually means they have watched a couple of programmes on television. You do actually know something.'

'A little but not enough. More than Helen anyway.'

He grinned and leaned forward.

'You and your friend are very different. Incidentally, did she know you were going to offer to pay for the meal last night?'

Adele shook her head vigorously. 'No. She would have thought I was mad and anyway I don't think she could afford it. She and her husband . . . '

She stopped abruptly but Michael was nodding.

'I saw the wedding ring but she didn't say anything about a husband so I thought she might be divorced or a widow.'

Adele explained about Helen and Roger.

'She really does love him but I don't think she appreciates how much it would hurt him to lose the shop. She just wants him to show her she is more important.'

He sighed.

'I'll give Tony a word of warning. He clearly likes her.'

'Well, perhaps a little admiration is

what she needs, so long as he'll settle for a holiday friendship and nothing more.'

'We'll see.'

Suddenly he stopped talking and swung his chair round, his eyes fixed on a young blonde girl who had walked past the café where they sat. He stared after her almost desperately and then shook his head and turned back to the table. The gaiety had disappeared, and once again he looked withdrawn and remote.

As the silence lengthened Adele said cautiously, 'Do you know that girl?'

He shook his head.

'No. I thought I did, but it's not her.'

Silence again. Wherever his thoughts were, they were not here in the sunlight of Kas, but Adele would not be shut out.

'Who did you think it was?'

'I thought it was Jenny,' he said, his voice full of despair.

She waited, but he seemed to think he had said enough.

'Jenny who?' she prompted, and he looked at her as if she were stupid not to know.

'Jenny, my sister.' With an obvious effort he tried to explain a little more. 'She disappeared. That's why Tony and I are here. We are trying to find her.'

Adele signalled to the waiter to bring fresh drinks and waited silently till they came. She pushed one towards Michael when he seemed unaware of its arrival till he picked it up and drank thirstily.

'Tell me about Jenny,' Adele encouraged him, and he sat back in his chair, ran his fingers through his hair, and began.

'There are just the two of us, Jenny and I. She's quite a bit younger than I am, just twenty. Maybe my parents and I have spoiled her because she is the youngest, because she is so pretty and lively, but we all love her dearly.'

He paused, and shut his eyes as if in pain.

'Jenny is at university, studying

Ancient History, and she decided to spend the Easter vacation in Turkey investigating some of the ancient ruins. We were all for this, because it seemed to show that she was finally taking her studies seriously as we had been worried that she was enjoying university life too much to spend a lot of time working. We understood she was going to a site which is being excavated by one of my father's old students, but when we didn't hear from her after two weeks we e-mailed him.

'He said he hadn't seen Jenny, though he had been expecting her. Then someone telephoned and asked to speak to Jenny. It turned out to be a boyfriend, someone called Nick. She met him at university, but we didn't know anything about him, and it was a big surprise when he told us that he and Jenny had planned to backpack around the country together. Then they had had a blazing row in Istanbul soon after they reached Turkey, though he didn't say what it was about.

He walked out and when he went back to their hotel the next day, Jenny had checked out without leaving a forwarding address. He assumed she had flown home, and he called us because he wanted to contact her.'

Michael stared ahead grimly.

'I dropped everything and flew to Turkey to find out what had happened to her. Tony managed to get some free time so he came with me. We found that Jenny checked out of the Istanbul hotel two hours after Nick left her. In spite of doing everything we can, we haven't heard from her and we haven't found anybody who has seen her since then. Tony and I came to Kas because she loved this place and we hoped she might come here, but so far there has been no trace of her.'

Adele tried to take in what he had told her. A young girl had disappeared and now her brother was desperately seeking for his beloved sister. No wonder Michael had been cold and distracted.

'Is it possible that she might have just gone off by herself and not told you? After all, she didn't tell you about the boyfriend.'

Michael shook his head.

'Jenny may not always tell us everything she's up to, but she has always been careful to tell us where she can be contacted. Our father has had a couple of health scares and she would want to know at once if he wasn't well.'

'What are you going to do next?'

'The Istanbul police said they would look out for her, but they obviously aren't going to put a girl who has had a row with her boyfriend high on their list of priorities. We think she has probably moved on or been taken elsewhere, if she is still alive. Kas is as good a place for me to stay as any. There are people here who know her from the times when we used to come with our parents. If they get news of her then they will tell me.'

Adele leaned forward and placed her

hand comfortingly over his.

'If I can help, you only need to ask.'

He smiled back at her gratefully, and she had the feeling that for the first time he was aware of her as a person.

3

As they walked back to the hotel, Michael continued to tell Adele more about the effort he'd put into trying to find his sister.

'I keep calling the police to make sure they keep looking for her and I have informed all the people I've contacted that there will be a reward for anyone who can give me information about her, but no-one has come forward yet.'

'What about money? Has her credit card been used?'

'She had quite a bit of cash because she and Nick planned to visit small towns and villages where it might not be easy to get money from banks, and she did draw out some more the day she left the hotel in Istanbul.'

'Has she got a mobile phone?'

'Yes, but there was no reply when we

called. That needn't mean anything. She was always running out of credit.'

She looked at him, examining his face carefully, noting the lines of strain and the dark shadows under his eyes.

'And what is this doing to you? How have you been able to come here to look for her? Have you taken time off from your work or what?'

'Fortunately I'm self-employed. I'm a consultant in engineering design, based in Cambridge, and I'd planned to take some holidays anyway, but if I don't find out what has happened to Jenny soon then life will get difficult.'

'And Tony?'

He smiled briefly.

'Tony's been my friend since we were at school together and he knows Jenny well. When I told him what had happened, he told his boss it was a family emergency and arranged for leave, but he'll have to go back soon as well. Sometimes I have nightmares that I'll never find out what has happened to Jenny. Not knowing what has happened to her is almost worse than having to cope with some disaster. At least I could go into action then.'

'So Tony tries to distract you by organising meals with strange women and arranging for you to take one sight-seeing,' she said ruefully, and he looked guilty.

'I'm afraid you're right.' His tone changed. 'But I really have enjoyed this morning. I didn't expect to, but I have, really.'

Back at the hotel, the receptionist told them that Tony and Helen were having lunch in the seaside snack bar a few yards away. They found them enjoying omelettes and a cool beer.

'Had a good morning?' Tony asked cheerfully, and then his face changed as he looked carefully at his friend. 'Have you told her?'

Michael nodded briefly. Adele shook her head when Helen looked up at her.

'I'll tell you later,' she told her quietly.

When they were back in their room after lunch, preparing to rest until the heat of the sun was less intense, Adele told Helen about Jenny, and her friend was full of ready sympathy.

'How dreadful! No wonder he was so offhand at first.'

They lay down on their beds. Adele had a book to read but she felt her eyelids growing heavy and put it down.

'Did you enjoy your old ruins?' Helen enquired sleepily.

'Very much. How did you and Tony get on?'

'Very well.' Helen giggled. 'He's fun. I told him about Roger and he agrees with me that I should come before the shop.'

Adele closed her eyes. She hoped that Michael would remember to explain to Tony that there was more than one side to the Helen and Roger story. Then she was asleep.

It seemed to be taken for granted that the four of them would go out together for dinner that evening, this time to a little restaurant down near the harbour.

'I insist we pay our share,' Adele said firmly as they prepared to order.

Tony made a token protest but Michael grinned.

'Good. If I haven't got to pay for you I can afford something special for myself.'

Now that they all knew about Jenny, the discussion over the meal was naturally about her. Tony seemed a bit more optimistic than Michael about a happy outcome.

'She's a wilful little madam,' Tony said cheerfully as he poured out more wine. 'She should have been spanked more often as a child.'

'That's not fair,' Michael protested, but his friend laughed at him.

'I know she's your darling little sister, but even you must remember some of the things she's got up to. She is perfectly capable of having gone off to stay somewhere with every intention of letting her family know where she is, but somehow never getting round to it.'

'Where would she go?'

'I don't know, but if she didn't tell you about the boyfriend, she may also have neglected to tell you about other people she knows. I trust she will appear safe and sound, but be prepared to give her a good telling-off when she does.'

His tone was light-hearted, but Adele could see that his eyes looked deeply troubled. She reflected that he was doing a lot for Michael out of friendship, and wondered how much he actually cared about the missing girl.

'My parents are flying to Dalaman in a couple of days and then coming here,' Michael said. 'I hope I'll have something to tell them by then.'

Michael certainly did all he could. While the two girls and Tony swam and lazed in the sun after breakfast the next day, he was busy telephoning and sending e-mails. The staff of the hotel all knew why he was there and did what they could to help, but even so, by mid-morning, he had done all he could for the day without gaining any useful information and could be seen pacing restlessly up and down along the hotel terrace.

'This frustration is driving him mad! Someone must know where she is!' Tony said impatiently, his eyes on his friend. 'She's a blonde English girl, so she will be noticeable wherever she is in Turkey, especially in the towns and villages.'

'I know you were being optimistic last night for Michael's sake, but what do you think has happened to her?' Adele enquired.

Tony shrugged.

'As I said last night, she could be staying with a friend, or just travelling around on her own. Those are the optimistic possibilities.'

'And the pessimistic possibilities?'

Tony's jaw clenched and he avoided looking at them.

'She may have been kidnapped in the hope of extracting a ransom from her family, or she may have been attacked and left for dead.'

There was a hush, and the sun seemed to lose its warmth for a second. Tony stirred irritably.

'I blame the boyfriend, Nick. He should never have walked out and left her on her own. She didn't know he would come back.'

Looking up, Adele saw Michael making his way down the steps towards them.

'Coming for a swim?' Tony asked him.

Whatever his fears, he would not let his friend see how worried he was. Michael shook his head.

'I thought I'd go along to the weekly market,' he told them. 'I need a few things. Would anyone like to come?'

'I will,' Adele said quickly. 'All I've to do is slip on my sundress and comb my hair.'

Soon she and Michael were climbing the steps to the road. Looking back, Adele saw Helen move closer to Tony and heard her laugh.

The market was like most small-town

markets, with stalls selling fruit and vegetables, crockery and pots and pans and various essentials. Michael bought some soap and razor blades and then they went on to look at stalls piled high with every possible colour of T-shirt.

As she turned away from one stall, she almost bumped into a small man in loose khaki trousers and a grey shirt. She drew back apologetically and the little man scuttled off. Adele looked after him, frowning.

'I'm sure I saw him near the hotel, and he was watching us while you were buying that soap,' she told Michael. 'Do you think he is following us?'

'Perhaps he wants to sell us a carpet,' he teased. 'I think it's time you got over this fear that every man in Turkey wants to sell you a carpet. To reassure you, I'm going to take you to meet a real carpet merchant.'

She hesitated.

'Don't you want to get back to the hotel? There might be some news.'

He patted his pocket.

'I've got my mobile phone and the hotel will contact me if I am needed.'

Together they climbed the steep, narrow streets until they came to a shop whose frontage was hung with richly-coloured carpets of many designs and sizes. Michael clapped his hands and a young man appeared, greeting him with cries of delight.

'Adele, meet Hassan,' Michael said laughingly. 'He knows a great deal about carpets and he has sold my family so many in the past that he dare not try to sell me any more.'

He turned to the young man.

'Hassan, show Adele your carpets and tell her something about them. Not the whole lecture — that can take hours!'

In an hour, after the ritual tea drinking, the charming Hassan managed to teach Adele quite a lot about the many kinds of carpet, the different dyes used, what the different patterns indicated, and the time taken to weave a good-quality carpet. She stroked a silk carpet that had taken years to make and felt something like awe.

'Do you feel you've learned much?' Michael asked her.

'Well, I think I can tell the difference between a good carpet and a bad one now,' she said thoughtfully, at which Hassan applauded her.

'That's a good beginning,' he said approvingly, and seemed genuinely regretful when Michael said that they had to leave.

At the door, he held Michael back for a moment, and Adele caught his whispered enquiry. 'Any news?' he asked and she saw his face fall when Michael shook his head.

Obviously he was one of the people in Kas who knew about Jenny. Adele halted abruptly as she and Michael began to walk back to the hotel.

'Look!' she said. 'There's the man we saw in the market. He must be following us!'

Michael looked and saw no-one.

'He hurried round the corner when I saw him.'

Michael was unworried.

'There are plenty of men who look and dress like him around here. Even if it is the same man, he may just be hoping to talk us out of a couple of pounds for something he is selling, or for showing us round Kas.'

'Then why doesn't he speak to us?'

Tactfully, Michael did not point out to her that the Turk might be proposing to show him certain sights or places that nice young ladies were not supposed to be interested in.

Lunch was once again in the snack bar, and it was agreed that they should all dine at a restaurant on the headland that protected the harbour. The afternoon was spent drowsing as usual as the sun beat down outside. After the girls had showered and prepared to go out, Helen checked her mobile for messages.

'Nothing,' she said tartly to Adele. 'He was supposed to meet that all-important buyer today, so it must have been a flop. I'm sure he would have called if he'd sold him a lot of the stock, just so he could tell me he was right to stay in England.' She tossed her hair. 'I don't care. I'm enjoying myself here.'

The air was warm, the sunset was spectacular, and the food was good, but somehow, the meal was not a complete success. Helen was too bright, drank a little too much and laughed a lot without any good reason. Michael was once again distracted with little attention to spare for his surroundings or companions, and it took all Tony's efforts to smooth over the difficult moments.

Helen hung on to Tony's arm as they strolled along by the water's edge after the meal, leaving Adele to walk with the silent Michael. Suddenly he sighed and turned to her.

'I'm sorry to be such bad company. I phoned my parents before I came out. My mother was very upset by the lack of news although I told her I am doing everything I can. I'm sure she thinks there must be something else, some-thing I've overlooked.'

'She knows you, so she knows you will do your best,' Adele reassured him.

He gave her a grateful smile and reached out for her hand, and their silence became more companionable. They took a taxi back to the hotel, where Tony and Helen got out and went into the reception area while Adele waited by the entrance as Michael paid off the driver.

As the taxi drove away, she was left momentarily alone, and suddenly she was aware of a figure darting out at her from a pool of darkness and briefly flinging his arms round her. Her bag fell from her grasp and she cried out in alarm, but as Michael ran to help her, the assailant was already racing away. As a street light shone on him, he looked back at Adele, and she realised that it was the little man whom she had seen in the market and outside Hassan's shop. Then he vanished into the shadows.

Tony and Helen heard her cry out and hurried back to her, but there was no sign of him. They had to accept that following him was hopeless and began to walk disconsolately back to the hotel. Michael stumbled on something and picked up an object lying on the roadway.

'It's your bag!' he said as Adele caught up with him.

She took it from him and then realised that she was shaking and was grateful when he put his arm round her protectively.

'It's shock. Let's go back to the hotel and get you a coffee.'

He peered into the darkness.

'There's nothing we can do. Even if we reported this to the police we can't find the man or say he took anything and we don't want to spend hours at the police station.'

Adele was vehement.

'I don't want any fuss! I've got my bag, so all I want now is that coffee, with plenty of sugar!'

They were soon safely inside the hotel, with Helen fussing over her friend while the two men fetched coffees. Adele laughed shakily.

'I'm all right now. It was just so unexpected.'

She drank her coffee when it came and felt better.

'I thought it was that same little man we saw in town, but, as you said, I can't prove it,' she said to Michael. 'But what was he trying to do? He didn't try to steal my bag.'

She felt in the pocket of her light jacket for her handkerchief and then stopped, frowning.

'Did he take anything?' Helen asked.

'No, nothing,' Adele said slowly, 'but this wasn't in my pocket before.'

She held out a crumpled piece of paper. Michael took it and smoothed it out, read what was on it, and then looked at it incredulously.

'What is it?' Tony said, and then, when he did not receive a reply he repeated the question more urgently.

'Michael, what is it?'

Michael looked up, his face white, and held out the sheet wordlessly. On it, printed crudely, were the words, *I can tell you what has happened to Jenny Brereton.*

'This was why he was following us,' Michael said slowly. 'He was looking for an opportunity to pass this to me or to Adele, because he'd seen us together.'

'Why give me the note? Why not speak to us?' Adele demanded.

Michael thought for a while.

'We've only seen him in busy places, like the market and the shopping area, and I would have grabbed him and made a fuss if he had told me then that he had information about my sister. He wants to speak to me somewhere away from other people. That's my guess, anyway.'

'Are you going to tell the police?' Tony asked.

Slowly, Michael shook his head.

'What could I say to them? I don't know who he is or where to look for him. Even if I did find him, he might just deny everything. No, when he gets in touch again I'll meet him wherever he wants me to. This is the first possible contact with anyone who claims to know what has happened to Jenny and I can't risk frightening him off.'

'Do you realise that he might bring friends with him to a meeting, that you will be putting yourself in danger?' Tony argued.

'Yes,' Michael said simply, 'but my mother was crying when I spoke to her tonight. I will take any risk that will help me to find Jenny.'

He held the little piece of paper as if it were something precious, Adele thought — and it was. It was the first tangible sign that he might yet find his sister.

4

Tony was breakfasting alone when Adele and Helen came down the next morning. He waved a piece of toast at them by way of greeting.

'Michael's gone already,' he said. 'He said the only thing he can do is wander slowly round the town so that the mysterious stranger can contact him if he wants to.'

Michael returned at lunchtime, dusty, tired and distinctly bad-tempered.

'I've stared into the window of every shop in Kas at least twice, I've shuffled slowly along all the roads and I've had half-a-dozen cups of coffee in different places, and I haven't seen that man anywhere. No urchin has tried to give me any messages, no matter how hopefully I looked at one. In fact all the mothers in Kas are probably warning everyone about the crazy Englishman.'

Tony gave an unsympathetic laugh, but at the same time pushed a cold beer towards his friend.

'Be patient. This time yesterday you were desperate because you'd heard nothing. You can wait a few more hours for the next development. He obviously wants to make contact, but he'll only do so when it feels safe. Now I heard you tossing and turning all last night, so have a good sleep this afternoon, then a swim, and then relax. Let him come to you when he is ready.'

Grudgingly, Michael let himself be guided by his friend, but his late afternoon swim did not last long.

'He can't contact me while I'm in the water,' he explained to Adele, throwing himself down beside her as she sunbathed.

She nodded, eyes closed, letting her body soak up the grateful warmth, but she could hear him shifting and sighing.

'Let's go for a walk,' he said abruptly. 'I can't just sit here any longer.'

Leaving Helen and Tony, they walked

along a coastal road that took them south out of Kas. There was little to say. Michael could think of nothing but the stranger who might lead him to his sister, so Adele wisely kept quiet and made no reply to his occasional angry comments on the situation. His pace grew faster and she was finding it difficult to keep up, until suddenly he stopped and gave a rather desolate laugh.

'I'm sorry! I shouldn't take my impatience and bad temper out on you.'

'There's no need to apologise. I understand how you feel,' she said tranquilly and he laughed again, but this time with genuine amusement.

'I really do believe you do, and I am grateful for your company. It does give Tony some respite from his constant attempts to make me feel better.'

He stretched out his hand.

'I didn't mean to walk you off your feet. Let's go and sit by the sea.'

They found their way down over some rocky ledges to a tiny sandy beach where they sat down.

'When are your parents arriving?' Adele enquired. 'They should be able to take some of the burden off you.'

'They've managed to get on a flight tomorrow,' he told her, 'but they won't be able to do much. My father has to be careful what he does because of heart trouble, and my mother looks after him. The responsibility for finding Jenny is mine.'

'What about boyfriend Nick? Doesn't he feel any responsibility? He was the one who left her alone in Istanbul.'

Michael's voice was rueful.

'Apparently not. Whatever the argument was about, their relationship is definitely over. Nick says Jenny made it impossible for him to stay. He seems to feel that if she is in trouble then it's her own fault.'

There seemed nothing else to say, and the two of them watched as the late afternoon light on the sea heralded the approach of dusk. As Adele looked out over the beach she found herself wishing that Jenny would appear safe and sound with some acceptable reason for her disappearance. That would leave Michael free to think of other things, such as possibly Adele herself. She was growing to like him very much and would have enjoyed spending the rest of a carefree holiday with him. Oh, well, even if Jenny did appear or was rescued, the Brereton family would probably catch the first available plane back to England.

A light evening breeze rippled across the sea and Adele shivered. Michael turned towards her.

'We'd better get back to the others and decide where we are going to eat tonight,' he remarked, glancing upwards.

Then he seemed to freeze. Sitting on top of a dune, looking down at them, was the man in the grey shirt and khaki trousers whom Michael had been looking for all day.

'Good evening,' the newcomer said in heavily-accented English as he approached them. 'This is a nice, quiet place, Mr Brereton. We can discuss your sister now.'

Michael made a movement to stand up, but the man's hand signalled him to stay where he was.

'I think it will be better if you remain at a distance,' the man continued. 'If you try to come any closer I will be gone before you can get up the dune. Now let us get down to business. You want to find your sister and I can help you.'

'Everybody in Kas knows that I am looking for my sister,' Michael said hotly. 'How can I be sure that you know anything useful?'

The man pulled something out of his pocket and dropped it down to the beach. Michael picked it up and stretched it between his hands so that Adele could see that it was a small, brightly-coloured scarf. She could tell that Michael recognised it from his bleak expression.

'Yes,' the stranger said smugly, 'it is your sister's. Accept that as proof, and listen to me. I have friends who are looking after Miss Brereton. She is perfectly safe with them at the moment, but if my friends begin to think that she is more trouble than she is worth, that you might be stupid enough to try to lead the police to them, for example, then they would not continue to be so kind.'

'How much do you want?' Michael asked roughly, and the small man nodded approvingly.

'Very sensible. Let us treat this as a business matter. You will be glad to hear that we know better than to ask the impossible. All we want is fifty thousand English pounds in used notes.'

'Fifty thousand pounds!'

'In used notes. A small price for your sister, we think. We know your father. He has savings and can borrow money. In fact we assume that as sensible people, you must have considered the possibility of a ransom demand and have already made enquiries about loans.'

Michael gestured helplessly.

'Perhaps we have, but such things take time to arrange, especially if you want used notes.'

The small man looked slightly bored.

'We realised that, of course. I shall expect you here in seven days, so you have a whole week to arrange matters. I think nine o'clock in the evening will be the best time.'

He stood up and dusted his trousers, obviously ready to leave.

'Stop!' Michael said urgently. 'If I can get the money and bring it here, what happens next?'

'An hour after I receive the money, Miss Brereton will be set free and told where to find you.'

As he turned away, Michael suddenly launched himself at the slope, scrambling up as fast as he could in a desperate attempt to follow the stranger who was vanishing in the half-light. Adele started to climb as well but slipped, twisting her ankle. Michael heard her cry of pain and turned back to her just as they heard the raucous sound of a motorbike starting up. As Michael hesitated, they saw the motorbike, heard it brake, and watched the small man fling himself on behind the rider. The motorbike was roaring away in the direction of the town in seconds.

'I'm sorry!' Adele told Michael. 'You should have gone on and left me.'

He shook his head and put his arm around her to support her as she hobbled towards the road.

'It was probably a good thing you did stop me. If I had caught him his friends would soon have got to know about it, and it might have put Jenny in danger. Now, lean on me as much as you like.'

Gratefully, she accepted his support. Her ankle was not badly hurt, but there was no point in putting unnecessary weight on it.

Back in Kas they told the other two what had happened.

'What will you do now?' Helen asked, wide-eyed.

'Start getting the money together. He

was right when he said we'd thought about ransom money. Fifty thousand pounds will make a big dent in my father's savings, but he has already contacted his bank about moving money over to Turkey. They don't know what the money is for, of course. I think he gave the impression that he was going to buy property over here.'

'Shouldn't you tell the police?' Tony said quietly. 'They will be furious if you get Jenny back and only then tell them about the ransom demands, when it will probably be too late to catch the men responsible.'

Michael looked undecided.

'It is a difficult decision, but I don't want to risk Jenny getting hurt. I'll go to the police when I don't feel I can get anywhere further by myself.' A brief smile appeared. 'At least I'll be able to tell my parents that I am making progress when I meet them at the airport.'

In their room that night, Helen obviously had something on her mind.

Eventually she turned to Adele.

'Michael believes that if he delivers the money then Jenny will be released. Suppose she's already dead? Has he thought of that?'

Adele recalled what had been said on the walk back to Kas.

'Of course he's aware of that possibility, but the kidnappers must know that if they kill a tourist, a young woman, they will be hunted down ruthlessly. Tourism is too important to Turkey for the country to risk visitors being scared away.'

She decided to change the subject.

'Michael is going to be busy with banks all day tomorrow. What shall we do?'

'Tony did say that there is a boat from the harbour that takes you to a beautiful little bay with clear water and even a snack bar for when you get hungry.'

Adele was just about to say that it sounded a very pleasant place to spend the day when Helen spoke again.

'It doesn't sound your kind of thing. You'd probably find it very dull.'

There was a world of meaning in her voice, and the message was clear.

'All right,' Adele said crossly. 'I know two's company and three's a crowd. I'll do some early souvenir shopping in Kas.'

Actually, she had to resist the impulse to give her friend a good shaking. Helen had invited her on this holiday under false pretences, had bored her stiff with her constant complaints about Roger, and now obviously preferred Tony's company to hers. Adele recalled that even at school Helen had had a ruthless streak when it came to getting her own way.

'We'll be spending the day together soon,' she reminded Helen. 'We booked an excursion to go and see Santa Claus's home, remember?'

'Yes,' Helen said gloomily. 'I thought it sounded like a theme park, and only found out too late that's it's another old church.'

Adele was still mildly annoyed with Helen the next morning, but did admit that it was quite pleasant to wander through the town by herself for a change. She had brought boxes of various exotic sweets and was wondering whether to stop for a coffee when she heard someone calling her.

'Miss Pearson! This way!'

It was Hassan, beckoning to her from the door of his carpet shop. He greeted her warmly.

'You can't just pass me by! You look as if you have been busy shopping so you must need a rest. Come in for some tea.'

It was very pleasing to her ego to be welcomed like this by a handsome young man after she had been abandoned by Helen, and she accepted his offer without hesitation and was soon seated by a low coffee table. An assistant brought the small glasses of tea while Hassan made sure that Adele was comfortably seated.

'Where is your friend? Where is

Michael?' he enquired, after he had inspected her purchases and assured her that she had made a wise choice.

'My friend wanted to go swimming and Michael is — er — busy,' she replied.

He caught the slight hesitation.

'Michael is busy?' He put his glass down and leaned forward. 'Busy about his sister? Is there any news?'

She explained while he listened eagerly. One point seemed to interest him especially.

'You say this small man followed you to my shop? That he was wearing khaki trousers and a grey shirt?'

'Well, he was outside when we left, and I think he probably followed us.'

Hassan's face was thoughtful.

'I think I have seem him. He has been hanging about for the past couple of weeks, not doing anything special. I thought he was probably doing odd jobs for shops and cafés.'

'He has a friend, someone who rides a motorbike.'

'I will ask around. Someone may know who he is or where he lives.'

Adele looked anxious.

'If he hears that people are asking questions about him it may cause trouble for Jenny.'

Hassan took her hand and patted it comfortingly.

'I would never do anything that might hurt Jenny. I will be very careful.'

Gazing into his dark eyes, Adele was sure she could trust him. After another glass of tea and some advice from Hassan on where to find the best shops, Jenny took her leave.

'Remember, you must call in and let me give you tea whenever you are near here,' Hassan told her. 'I like having a beautiful young lady as my guest.'

It was outrageous flattery and she laughed at him, but his open admiration had made her feel much better and she returned to the hotel in a happier mood.

Helen, however, was distinctly bad-tempered when she and Tony returned about tea-time. The bay had been beautiful, but she had been bored.

'All Tony talked about was this girl, Jenny,' she complained. 'Then he stopped talking altogether when I asked him why he was so concerned about her and I told him he should leave Michael to worry about his sister.'

She peered anxiously into the mirror.

'I was in the sun for too long, too. I've got burned, and the snack bar didn't have much choice. Then there was a wind blowing on the way back and the boat was rolling about so much that I was afraid it would sink!'

Adele, refreshed by a relaxing afternoon by herself, made sympathetic noises but secretly felt that Helen had deserved to suffer.

Michael returned, alert and invigorated after a day spent meeting with various financial people. The experience of actually having something useful to do had clearly been good for him, but in spite of his high spirits, dinner was a lacklustre meal. Helen was sulking very obviously and Tony hardly said a word. When they had finished, Helen pushed back her chair and announced that she was tired and was going back to the hotel at once.

'I'll go with you,' Tony said hastily.

Helen looked at him frostily.

'I'm not sure I want company. I've had a hard day,' she said. 'Adele will come back with me.'

'Actually, I wanted to talk to Michael,' Adele said.

Helen bit her lip, and she and Tony set off back to the hotel, with a careful distance left between them.

'What on earth is the matter with them?' Michael wondered.

'A slight difference of opinion on what makes a good day, I'm afraid,' Adele said wryly.

'Let's forget about them. I'll order coffee for us and then you can tell me what you want to talk about.'

'I saw Hassan today,' Adele began, and went on to recount how Hassan was going to see if he could find out anything about the small man. 'I was afraid you might think I'd done the wrong thing by telling him what had happened,' she confessed, but Michael shook his head firmly.

'You can rely on Hassan. He can be very discreet and now, when he knows Jenny's safety is at stake, he will be very careful indeed. In fact he could be extremely useful. As he said, he knows everyone in the town.'

Adele relaxed and decided to enjoy the remainder of the evening. Once again the silver ripples on the water reflected the moonlight and the stars seemed twice as big as they did in England.

'Would you like some more coffee or a liqueur?' Michael enquired.

'No, thank you, but why don't you have a liqueur or a brandy?'

'You know I don't like brandy.'

'No, I don't. Why should I? I've only known you for a few days.'

He looked at her blankly and then laughed.

'I'm sorry. You're right, of course. It's just that I seem to have known you for ages, yet in fact we know very little about each other.'

She smiled at him.

'I've changed my mind. I'll have another cup of coffee and then we can learn more about each other.'

He told her more about his work and she explained that though she hoped to do well when she was a fully-fledged accountant, as a trainee living in a bed-sitter in London she was far from rich.

'That's why I was so relieved when you refused to take the money for that dinner,' she confessed.

It was another hour before they left the restaurant, and they walked back to the hotel like old friends.

5

Michael seemed to take it for granted that Adele would come to the airport with him to meet his parents. At first she was mildly surprised, then flattered and rather pleased. This holiday was proving very different from what she had imagined it would be, but now she was deeply involved in the Brereton family problems. Anyway, Helen would not miss her, as she and Tony had somehow been reconciled on their walk back to the hotel.

Michael had booked a room for his parents at a large hotel a little distance away. It had more lifts and fewer stairs than the one they were staying at, and he had managed to secure a large room on the ground floor, very suitable for his father's health.

It was a long drive to the airport in the hired car but Adele almost wished it longer. The narrow, twisting roads ran through dramatic scenery and Michael seemed to know every inch of the way, his comments ranging from information about ancient people to memories of walks with his parents when he was young.

'It sounds like a very happy childhood,' she said wistfully.

'It was,' he agreed, and looked at her sharply. 'Why? Wasn't yours?'

She shook her head.

'I'm afraid not. My mother was always hopeless with money, and she and my father had constant rows about it. My father walked out one day when I was ten, and my mother died when I was just fifteen. I spent the next few years with her parents, who resented having their plans for a quiet retirement disrupted by a teenager.'

'And then you became an accountant.'

'Yes. A quiet, well-ordered existence, probably a reaction against my childhood.'

'Yet Helen is your best friend? She is very different from you.'

'Opposites attract. Occasionally she envies me my peaceful, risk-free life, and sometimes I envy the excitement and uncertainty of her life.'

'Do you think she will go back to her husband?'

'I really hope so. I like him and I think he is good for her.'

The airport was busy with groups of tourists being shepherded to their coaches by travel reps and Michael's parents were virtually the last people to emerge from the terminal. Adele recognised them at once. Mr Brereton looked like an older Michael, but with a shock of white hair, and Michael had clearly inherited his mother's dark eyes.

Michael introduced Adele briefly, picked up the luggage, and escorted them out to where the car stood in the blazing sunshine. Mr Brereton started to interrogate Michael almost as soon as they were out of the carpark, wanting to know everything he had done and what responses he had received. He had several criticisms to make, each of which Michael answered patiently. At last there was nothing more to ask, and the last hour of the journey was spent in silence. Mrs Brereton had hardly said a word the whole time, so Adele had no way of knowing how she felt about the unexpected presence of an unknown young woman.

When they arrived at the hotel, Mr Brereton inspected the bedroom Michael had reserved, gave it approval grudgingly, and then insisted on taking Michael off to the lounge where he obviously intended to question him again. Left by themselves, the two women looked at each other uncertainly.

'Can I help you unpack and hang clothes up?' Adele said politely and was rewarded with an uncertain smile.

'Would you be so kind? I feel exhausted after the journey,' Mrs Brereton confessed.

They worked together for some minutes, and were then disturbed by a knock on the door which signalled the arrival of a tea tray. Gladly, they abandoned the unpacking and sat down. Mrs Brereton drank her tea gratefully and then turned to Adele.

'My husband must have made a bad impression on you,' she said.

Adele shook her head politely and murmured a vague denial but the other woman clearly didn't believe her.

'He isn't usually like this, but he wishes he could take charge of the search for Jenny, and he can't. The doctors have told him he must avoid stress as much as possible so he has got to leave everything to Michael and it is so frustrating for him.'

'I understand. Michael is very like him, and he is also feeling frustrated because he hasn't made more progress. But he is doing everything he can, and I am sure his father will realise that,' Adele assured her, and the other woman relaxed slightly.

'Michael said you are a friend. Did you know him in England?'

'We met in Kas only a few days ago, but — yes — I think we are friends.'

Mrs Brereton was looking at her now with more interest.

'A few days ago? It usually takes Michael weeks to decide that he likes someone!'

Adele realised that she was blushing.

'Well, these aren't normal circumstances. As soon as I heard about Jenny I wanted to help, of course . . . '

Her voice trailed off as she asked herself if she would have been so eager to help if Michael had been fifty years old and fat!

Tactfully, Mrs Brereton did not ask any more questions and soon after that Michael and his father returned. Mr Brereton must have been satisfied with the results of his interrogation for he was in a much better mood and even thanked Adele for her help before she and Michael left.

'Do you realise that we haven't had any lunch?' Michael asked as he held the car door open.

'Actually, I have been feeling more and more aware of the fact,' Adele confessed, and he grinned at her.

'Well, I didn't feel like having lunch with my parents. I love them dearly, but at the moment I don't want to answer any more questions.'

Back at their own hotel, there was no sign of Helen or Tony, so the two of them had a snack lunch by the sea. Helen had still not reappeared when Adele woke up from her afternoon siesta and showered, but she was not worried. After all, Helen had Tony to look after her. She was not likely to vanish like Jenny.

There were no other guests in the lounge when she came down, so she smiled at the receptionist and then sank down in a comfortable chair to enjoy a few minutes peacefully gazing out over the sea. There was the sound of light footsteps coming up the steps from the street and Adele looked round to see a girl of about twenty entering the hotel. She looked tired and her light blouse and jeans were creased, her blonde hair tousled. Noting the pack on her back, Adele decided that she must have just arrived on the Dalaman bus, and pitied her the long journey in the afternoon heat.

She turned back to the view, but heard the girl's clear voice as she addressed the receptionist.

'Have you got a room free? A single room?'

There was a polite murmur from the receptionist as she checked the room situation. The girl, obviously conscious of her rather bedraggled state, spoke again with a defensive note in her voice.

'I have stayed here before, with my family, more than once.'

'Then we are flattered that you decided to come back,' the receptionist said politely. 'We do have a single room, though I am afraid it does not have a sea view.'

'I'll take it.'

The receptionist reached for a form. 'And your name?'

'My name is Jenny Brereton.'

The receptionist looked up sharply and Adele's chair crashed into the wall as she thrust it back and stood up. The newcomer found both Adele and the receptionist staring at her.

'What's the matter?' the girl said nervously.

Now Adele moved swiftly so that she was between the girl and the exit. If this was an impostor, sent for some reason by the kidnappers, she would not let her escape.

'You say you are Jenny Brereton. Have you got a brother?'

The girl nodded.

'Yes. He's called Michael.'

'Can you prove you are Jenny Brereton?'

Deeply bewildered, but aware of the tension in the air, the girl fumbled in her bag and brought out a passport which she handed to Adele without a word. With shaking fingers, Adele found the page with the name and identifying photograph and checked the picture against the passport's owner. There was no doubt. This was Jenny Brereton. She pushed the passport back into the girl's hand and turned to the receptionist.

'Quick! Call him!'

The young blonde was edging near the door.

'I don't know what's the matter, but if I'm not wanted here . . . '

Adele clutched her by the wrist as the receptionist spoke frantically into the telephone.

'No! You've got to stay till your brother comes!'

The girl shook her head desperately.

'Let me go! You've got the wrong person. My brother is in England.'

'He's upstairs. He's been trying to find your kidnappers.'

Now the girl looked scared and was struggling to get away, clearly convinced she was in the grip of a mad woman, but before she could break free there was a shout from the stairs.

'Jenny!'

Michael stood there, wearing only his jeans, bare-chested and barefoot, his hair still wet. He had obviously still been in the shower when the telephone rang. For a few seconds there was complete silence as nobody moved. Then the girl flung herself towards the steps as Michael rushed to greet her. He embraced her tightly and held her to him, rocking her in his arms.

'Where have you been? Are you all right? Did you escape or did they let you go?' he demanded as he finally released her.

His sister looked at him wildly.

'What do you think has been happening? Why are you here? And who is she?'

This final question was accompanied by a finger stabbing towards Adele. Michael took a deep breath, but held on to his sister's hands as if he was afraid she would vanish if he let her go for an instant. He looked at Adele.

'Please, would you go and bring my parents here? Tell them what has happened, but break it to them gently.'

As Adele nodded and made for the street, she heard Jenny say plaintively,

'You mean our parents are here as well? It sounds as if I'm in deep trouble. And I'm desperate for a cup of coffee!'

★　★　★

Adele knocked on the door of the Breretons' room three times before they answered. Obviously they had been asleep, resting after their journey. It was Mrs Brereton, wrapped in a light dressing-gown, who opened the door and stared in amazement at Adele, who was still panting after her desperate rush from one hotel to the next.

'What's the matter?'

'Can I come in?'

Mrs Brereton cast a glance over her shoulder at the interior of the room and then evidently decided that it was fit to receive visitors and stepped back, allowing Adele to enter. Her husband was coming out of the bathroom in shirt and trousers, vigorously towelling his face, but he stopped when he saw Adele.

'Is something wrong? Has there been bad news?'

Adele tried to smile reassuringly. She didn't want Jenny's sudden appearance to give her father a heart attack.

'Not at all. Can we sit down?'

She took an upright chair while the Breretons perched on the edge of one of the beds and looked at her expectantly. She saw that Mr Brereton was gripping his wife's hand tightly.

'I was sitting in the lounge of our hotel,' she began with careful casualness, 'when someone came in off the street and asked for a room.'

She saw Mr Brereton move impatiently. Perhaps to keep him in suspense would be more stressful than just telling him the facts.

'It was Jenny,' she said.

They looked at her uncomprehendingly.

'Jenny,' she repeated, 'your daughter. She's there with Michael now. Apparently she hasn't been kidnapped after all.'

She saw amazement and then relief

on their faces. Suddenly Mrs Brereton burst into sobs and her husband turned to hold her.

'Leave us now,' he said quietly to Adele. 'It will take us a few minutes to get ready. Wait for us in the reception area here, please.'

She was relieved that he had taken the news so calmly, and then she saw the beads of perspiration standing out on his forehead.

It was a good quarter of an hour before they appeared, dressed for the street. Mrs Brereton's face was shining with excitement, but her husband's was carefully non-committal. Adele described Jenny's unexpected appearance during the short walk to her own hotel, where they found Michael and Jenny waiting for them in the lounge.

Michael was now wearing a T-shirt and sandals as well as his jeans, and Jenny had combed her hair. Whatever Michael had said to her during Adele's absence had made Jenny look very apprehensive, but at the sight of her parents she rushed to embrace them and all three hugged each other tightly while Michael and Adele watched.

Finally, amid kisses and tears of joy, the Breretons sank down round a table while Michael ordered cool drinks for them all. Adele decided that although this was a family occasion she had been sufficiently involved in the search for Jenny to justify her staying to find out what had actually happened to the girl. She did not have to wait long before explanations were being demanded.

'It's all been a big misunderstanding,' Jenny told them, then looked at their faces and hurried on. 'All right, I didn't tell you that Nick was coming to Turkey with me because I didn't want you jumping to conclusions or making a fuss. Anyway, by the time we got to Istanbul I had decided I had made a big mistake, and I told him I wanted him to go away and leave me.'

Adele felt a pang of sympathy for the much-maligned Nick. Why couldn't Jenny have realised she'd made a mistake before they left England?

'He refused to believe me at first, but then he stormed out in a temper.' Jenny looked at her parents guiltily. 'Perhaps I should have flown home then, but I felt I'd made a fool of myself and I didn't want to face you and admit that. I called a Turkish girl, a student at the university who is a friend of mine, and she invited me to go and stay with her and her family. So I did. That's where I've been all this time. Then I decided to come to Kas, for old times' sake, and use it as a base for exploring some of the ruins.'

'Why didn't you tell us where you were? Why didn't you call us?' Michael said with an edge to his voice, but his sister stared at him indignantly.

'I did! I ran out of credit on my phone so I went to an internet café and sent you an e-mail.'

'We never received it,' Mr Brereton began, but Michael interrupted.

'Jenny, you know perfectly well you are always putting in e-mail addresses incorrectly and that even one wrong letter stops them being delivered. Did you wait and check that it had not been returned undelivered?'

Jenny's cheeks burned hotly as she shook her head.

'I had a bus to catch. I just pressed **Send** and ran out of the café.'

There was silence, until Mr Brereton stirred and sighed gustily.

'So we have all been panicking, your mother and I have been worried sick, Michael and Tony dropped everything and flew out here, just because you couldn't be bothered to check whether an e-mail had been delivered or not.'

Jenny sat up sharply.

'Tony's here?'

'He came with me in case I needed help. In fact, he's been trying to keep me sane over the past days,' Michael said wearily.

Jenny was frowning.

'What was all that stuff about being kidnapped?'

She glared at Adele.

'That girl was talking some nonsense and holding me so tightly that she's bruised my wrists!'

'We were told that you had been kidnapped,' her brother said.

'Who told you that?'

'The kidnapper,' Michael said with careful patience, and then looked startled. 'But he couldn't have been the kidnapper because you were never kidnapped.'

He drew the little silk scarf from his pocket.

'He gave us this scarf as proof that he and his friends were holding you.'

'I wondered what had happened to that. I thought I'd left it in the hotel in Istanbul.'

'Perhaps you did and someone found it. Then, when I started making enquiries, I suppose they saw how they could use it to support what they said if they claimed that they had kidnapped you,' Michael said slowly.

His face grew thunderous.

'Wait till I see that little man again!'

As the Breretons contemplated the way they had been deceived, the noise of voices and laughter were heard, and Tony and Helen entered. Jenny stood up, her eyes shining.

'Tony!'

He turned towards her, startled, as she smiled at him.

'Tony! I'm here, safe. I wasn't kidnapped. I just went to stay with a friend for a while.'

He stared at her, his face darkening.

'You stupid little girl!' he burst out. 'Michael and I have been desperately searching for you, the police are involved, and the worry might have killed your father. And all the time you've been staying with a friend. You silly, selfish, little fool!'

Turning his back on her, he made for the stairs. Stunned, Jenny burst into tears, and as her mother agitatedly tried to comfort her, Adele saw a small secret smile on Helen's face.

6

'So the silly girl has been staying with a friend and leaving her family to worry,' Helen commented, leaning casually back in her chair.

'She thought they knew where she was,' Adele said patiently.

Helen seemed intent on seeing Jenny in the worst possible light.

'She made one attempt at contacting them, didn't check, and then forgot all about them. No wonder Tony was so angry!'

Adele's lips tightened.

'I don't understand Tony's reaction. Her family is delighted to have her back, so why was he so unpleasant? After all, he must care about her. He came out to help Michael look for her.'

Helen shrugged.

'I think he may have had a fondness for her in the past, but not now she has shown how immature she is. He's obviously fed-up with her. I hope he's decided he likes me more. I certainly like him.'

'Helen! Stop talking like that! You're married, or have you forgotten Roger?'

'He seems to have forgotten me,' Helen said bitterly. 'I'm free to find someone else.'

'You mean you want to be reassured that even if Roger doesn't want you, someone else does.'

Helen looked at her coldly.

'You've spent plenty of time this holiday with Michael Brereton, leaving me with Tony, so you can't blame me if we've grown close. I like to have a man around. You wouldn't know about that, because you've never managed to keep one. Tomorrow I'll make sure that Tony decides his future is with me.'

They left the restaurant where they had been dining and went back to the hotel and to bed in icy silence. There was no sign of the Breretons or of Tony. Adele lay awake for some time, her mind full of what had happened during the day. She was sure that Helen was awake as well, but when she whispered her friend's name there was no response. Finally she fell asleep, but her rest was disturbed by dreams and she woke late to find that Helen had already left the room.

There were no familiar faces at breakfast, and the receptionist told her that Mr Tony had said he was taking the ferry to an island, and that Adele's friend had gone with him. Disconsolately, Adele wandered along the sea front. She was extremely annoyed with Helen. She also felt abandoned by everyone. The Breretons would be busy as a family, and she had no claim on their attention.

She walked slowly along to the town. Determined to enjoy at least part of the day, she made her way to Hassan's shop, feeling that a little attention and flattery was just what she wanted, but there was no sign of him as she hesitated outside, so she drifted back to the hotel, went for a swim and had a snack lunch, and then caught up with some of her sleep during the afternoon's heat.

There was no sign of Helen when she woke, so she had a long shower and spent an unusual amount of time choosing what to wear and then sat on the balcony reading till the sun was setting. By this time she felt hungry, and told herself firmly that she did not need company to enjoy herself. She would go back to the Mermaid restaurant and treat herself to a good dinner.

Adele was flattered when the waiter remembered her, but when he led her into the restaurant he did not take her to an empty table. Instead he led her to one already occupied by four people, the Brereton family! Obviously he remembered her and took it for granted that she had come to join Michael. Adele halted and tried to smile, but felt extremely embarrassed. They would think she was forcing herself on their family gathering.

Michael was the first to see her and he stood up, drawing the attention of the others to her.

'Adele! What a pleasant surprise!'

He looked past her, obviously expecting to see her followed by someone else, then looked back at her questioningly.

'Is Helen with you?'

She shook her head.

'Helen has been out all day.'

He looked as if he were going to ask another question, but contented himself with saying, 'But you can't have dinner by yourself. Come and join us.'

'I don't want to intrude. I didn't expect to find you here.'

'Nonsense, you're very welcome.'

This time it was Mrs Brereton speaking.

'After all, you were the one who actually found Jenny.'

The waiter was already drawing a chair out for her, so Adele sat down. Michael smiled at her.

'As a reward, Adele, I'll pay for your dinner.'

His mother looked at him in some surprise, and he grinned.

'A private joke, Mother.'

In fact, it was a pleasant, relaxed evening. Now they no longer had to worry about Jenny, the Breretons were obviously enjoying their return to their old haunts. Adele gathered that they intended to stay for a few more days and she listened to their plans to revisit their favourite spots. Jenny was a little subdued. Possibly she was still coming to terms with the trouble her disappearance had caused.

Nobody mentioned Tony.

As they walked back to the hotel, Michael laid a hand lightly on her arm and slowed down so that they were a little behind the others.

'Do I take it that Tony is with Helen?' he asked quietly.

She nodded, and looked at him anxiously.

'I'm worried. I think Helen is leading him on because she's angry with Roger, not because she has really fallen for Tony.'

In the dim light, she saw Michael grimace.

'I don't know why he acted as he did last night. He wouldn't talk to me about it afterwards.'

'Well, let's hope they have spent the day discussing their troubles with each other and have sorted things out,' Adele said with attempted lightness.

Mr and Mrs Brereton turned off to their hotel and the remaining three made their way back to theirs. The keys to both Adele's and Michael's rooms had already been taken, indicating that Tony and Helen were back. Adele climbed the stairs slowly, wondering what she would do if the door were locked against her, but the handle turned and the door opened without any difficulty. The room beyond was in darkness.

'Helen?' she whispered, wondering if her friend was possibly asleep.

There was no reply, but she thought she heard the bed creak.

'Helen?' she repeated more loudly,

and this time she distinctly heard not only movement but also a noise that sounded like a suppressed sob.

Adele switched on the light. Helen was curled up on her bed, fully dressed, with her eyes red and her face blotchy. Their differences were instantly forgotten as Adele hurried to take her friend in her arms. Helen immediately burst into tears, and for some time Adele sat holding her and murmuring to her comfortingly, until Helen finally pulled herself upright, blew her nose, and looked at her friend tragically.

'I've made a complete fool of myself! Tony didn't want me.'

Adele felt immense relief sweep through her, but continued to make soothing noises.

'Roger doesn't want me! Tony doesn't want me! Nobody loves me!'

Helen's voice rose to a wail, but Adele wanted facts, not melodrama.

Swiftly she went to her suitcase and found the duty-free bottle of brandy she had bought on the plane and had intended to take home with her. She poured two generous helpings into their tooth-glasses and handed one to Helen.

'Drink that and tell me what happened,' she commanded.

Obediently, Helen sipped some brandy and then stared at Adele forlornly.

'We had a lovely day. Tony never mentioned Jenny and he was paying me all kinds of compliments. We decided to have a meal on the island and catch the last ferry back.'

She sniffed.

'Maybe I drank more than I usually do, but Tony just went on flirting when I expected him to get serious, so in the end I started hinting and when that didn't have any effect, I told him straight out that I found him very attractive and was willing to, to . . . '

This time the sniff sounded indignant.

'I didn't say anything that was any more suggestive but I might as well have done. He stared at me for a while, looking absolutely silly, and then gulped and said that he was sorry if he'd given me the wrong impression, that he really liked me, but only as a friend!'

She drank some more brandy.

'Then I had to pretend that he had misunderstood me, though we both knew he hadn't. The ferry ride back to Kas was horrible. We just sat there, careful not to touch each other, walked back to the hotel with at least a yard between us, and were glad when we got to the hotel and could separate. What do I do now, Adele?'

'There's not much you can do except resolve not to make a fool of yourself another time. We've only a few days left, so you and Tony can probably avoid each other, and he may be going back to England before us, anyway.'

'We can't avoid each other all the time! What about breakfast?'

'Smile, and keep quiet. And now, if you don't mind, I want to go to bed. It has been a long day, most of it rather boring, and I want some sleep.'

When Adele woke in the morning,

Helen was still asleep. There were shadows under her eyes and she moved restlessly from time to time. Adele washed and dressed quietly and left her friend to sleep. Tony was the only familiar face at breakfast and he looked as though he had not slept at all. He managed to scrape up a welcoming smile as Adele sat down.

'Have you got plans for today?' she asked him cheerfully, but he shook his head.

'I'll probably go to the travel agent's to confirm my flight back to England in a couple of days. Now that Jenny has reappeared safe and sound there is no reason for me to stay here any longer.'

He seemed about to say something else, then stopped, and she looked at him enquiringly.

'What's the matter?'

'Nothing,' he said lamely, but then added hurriedly, 'How is Helen?'

Adele laid down her knife and fork.

'Very upset,' she said sternly.

'What did she say?'

'Not much beyond pleading with me to get her some aspirins. As far as I can make out, the two of you had a bit too much to drink last night and she has an awful headache this morning. She also has a vague feeling that something embarrassing happened, but she can't remember what it was, and that's worrying her.'

Relief was clearly visible on Tony's face as he saw the escape route she was offering him.

'You're right. We did have too much to drink, and my memory is very blurred as well. You can tell Helen that if something awkward did happen, I can't remember it either.'

By the time he left the breakfast table, he looked much happier and Adele went back to check on Helen, who was awake and dressed.

'It's safe to come down,' she reported. 'Just remember that you and Tony had too much wine last night and neither of you can remember what you said to each other. Tony is on his way to confirm his ticket home, anyway, so you probably won't see much of him before he goes.'

Helen looked as relieved as Tony had done, but then her woebegone expression returned.

'I should have listened to you, Adele. You always know best. Why was I so stupid?'

Adele's heart sank as she saw herself doomed to listen to a repentant and breast-beating Helen for the rest of the day. Fortunately, when they went downstairs, they found the whole Brereton family assembled. A minor argument was in progress because Mrs Brereton wanted to go shopping and her daughter was refusing to accompany her.

'You spend ages in a shop and then quite often you don't buy anything. It's embarrassing!' Jenny told her mother.

'But I don't want to go on my own!'

Adele saw an escape route.

'Why don't you and Helen go shopping together?' she said brightly to

Mrs Brereton. 'Helen loves shopping.'

It took a little time, but Helen was persuaded that she would be doing a good deed if she accompanied Mrs Brereton, a good deed, Adele managed to imply, which would somehow go some way to compensating for her recent behaviour. Finally Mrs Brereton and Helen set off together, followed by Michael and Mr Brereton, who wanted to visit a surprisingly good antique shop in the resort. Jenny and Adele were left free to go swimming.

After an hour or so, they adjourned for morning coffee. Jenny was obviously preoccupied by something.

'I haven't seen Tony today,' she said, failing completely to make it sound like a casual remark.

'He was going to make sure of his flight home,' Adele informed her, and Jenny's face fell. She drank half her coffee and then sighed. Adele ignored this, so Jenny sighed again, deeply this time. Adele did not feel in the mood to receive any more confidences and continued to drink her coffee placidly, so Jenny tried a more direct approach.

'I suppose you have been wondering why I've behaved so badly,' she began, but Adele shook her head firmly.

'It's nothing to do with me,' she replied. 'It's your family who is entitled to know.'

But Jenny was obviously intent on confession.

'I'm not sure they would understand, but another girl might.'

Adele gave in. After all, she was actually quite curious about Jenny's reasons for disappearing.

'Tell me,' she said, and Jenny began.

'My family, even Michael, still treat me as if I were a little girl. But I'm not. I'm old enough to fall in love, and that's what I did. I fell in love with Tony, but he just sees me as Michael's little sister. Then, when I was feeling really miserable about this, I met Nick at college and he obviously thought I was very attractive. I was flattered, and he was good-looking. I suppose I thought that Tony might think of me differently if he realised that another man admired me, so when I decided to come to Turkey I asked Nick if he would like to come as well.'

She gave Adele an uncomfortable look.

'Up to then, we'd been out together a few times, but that's all.'

'You mean you hadn't slept together,' Adele said directly, and Jenny blushed deeply.

'Yes, that is what I mean. I was stupid and naive. Some people I know have travelled together without being lovers, but Nick wasn't thinking of that. Anyway, when we got to Istanbul and checked into the hotel, he tried to make love to me, and I panicked. I wanted Tony, no-one else. So I threw an awful scene and told Nick to get out, and as soon as he'd gone I called my friend, packed and left. And I did think the e-mail had got through to my family!'

She was looking a little tearful.

'And then, when I saw Tony here, he

was so furious with me! He obviously thinks I'm just a stupid little fool, and he will never care for me now!'

Adele was inclined to agree with this, but she could not say so to Jenny.

'Well, I think he was upset by the worry you'd caused your family,' she said cautiously.

'But what can I do to show him that I won't do anything like that again?' Jenny pleaded, and Adele found she had little comfort to offer.

'Give him time,' was all she could say. 'Show him you can be sensible and eventually you will be friends again. But you may have to accept that he will never care for you in the same way as you care for him.'

Obviously this was not what Jenny wanted to hear, but she bit her lip and nodded, and soon afterwards both girls slipped back into the water.

Adele and Helen joined the Breretons for lunch. The shopping expedition had obviously been a great success as Mrs Brereton and Helen had found that they were soul mates when it came to shopping and had thoroughly enjoyed themselves, returning with quite a number of well-filled bags. Michael was busy teasing Helen and his mother and had little to say to Adele.

Tony appeared late, greeted Adele and the older Breretons with apparent cheerfulness, but avoided looking at Helen or Jenny.

'Did you get your flight confirmed?' Adele asked him, and he nodded.

'I've got a seat on a plane back to London the day after tomorrow.'

Adele saw Jenny's eyes widen in horror when she heard this, though she said nothing.

Helen was pleasantly exhausted by her shopping trip and later that afternoon, Adele was able to leave her still sound asleep when she quietly left their room. She had decided she wanted a couple of hours to herself, away from the problems of the Breretons and Helen. She would follow the shore road for a couple of miles, enjoying the view and think of nothing in particular.

She should have refused, therefore, when she met Michael at the bottom of the stairs and he asked her if she would like to come for a walk. Instead she found herself agreeing. After all, Michael was fairly problem-free and he did know the area. She did not analyse her reasons for accepting beyond that.

'Let's go up behind the town,' he suggested. 'You soon get into open country and there are some marvellous views.'

He neglected to mention that the walk began with a steep climb, but when Adele turned to look back over the sea she felt it was worthwhile. Kas itself was partly hidden, but the bay and nearby islands made a colourful panorama. Continuing to climb and passing by one or two small farms, they found themselves walking through fields filled with flowers.

'This is probably the best time of the year,' Michael told her. 'The plants are all in a hurry to flower before it gets too hot and dry.'

Finally they reached the crest of the hill and sank down to rest. The view had expanded, new vistas had appeared, and Adele felt she had rarely seen anything so beautiful.

7

For some time Adele sat gazing out over the sea, absorbing the beauty spread out below her and glad of the opportunity to forget all the petty affairs and complications that waited back in Kas. But when she looked at Michael, he was frowning at the ground. He saw her staring at him and smiled apologetically.

'I'm sorry. It's just a problem that is worrying me.'

'I thought all your problems were solved now that Jenny has reappeared. Instead you're still worried about something. What is it?'

'You may be able to give me some good advice. There's this man, and he's had an argument with a girl . . . '

He stopped and drew a deep breath.

'Oh, well, I might as well tell you everything. It's Tony. You know how he reacted when he saw Jenny at the hotel, how rude he was to her? Well, when we went up to our room, I told him that I was disgusted by the way he behaved and I couldn't understand why, but he refused to talk about it. Then, last night when he came back, he told me he was in love with her! He said that when he saw Jenny at the hotel he was overjoyed but angry at the same time, and it was the anger that showed.'

Michael's tone, one almost of shock, made it clear that Tony's confession had come as a complete surprise.

'In fact, he said that he realised how he felt about her some months ago, but he just didn't know how to tell her. She has always regarded him as a friend, to both of us, and he couldn't think how to change the relationship and he couldn't tell in me in case I disapproved. He didn't know how to behave, so he started to avoid her! In fact, Jenny did ask me once why he was behaving so oddly.'

Adele thought back to her talk with

Jenny. If Tony had only told her how he felt back in England then how much simpler things would have been!

'How would you have reacted if your friend had told you he had fallen for your little sister?'

Michael obviously thought this was a stupid question.

'I'd have been delighted! They would make a good pair, balancing each other. Tony is sensible and down-to-earth while Jenny would bring him a sense of adventure and excitement. When she took off for Turkey with Nick, Tony thought he'd lost her anyway. Then she disappeared, and he was obviously as desperate to find her as I was. Now he has upset Jenny and feels he has no chance of ever patching things up with her. Even when we all get back to England he can't believe she will ever want to see him again.'

Adele could not betray Jenny's confidences, but she decided she could hint at the truth.

'You know, I think Jenny was so upset

because she cares more about Tony than he realises.'

'You mean she might feel the same way about him as he does about her?'

Adele decided she had said enough.

'You could just tell her how he feels and see how she reacts.'

'Exactly how do I bring the subject up? Do I just say, 'By the way, I know Tony said you were a stupid little fool, but that was because he is in love with you'?'

'Why not?'

'Because there is the extra complication, that since she reappeared, he has been doing his best to give the impression that he is very interested in your friend, Helen. He may not be serious about her, but Jenny must have got a very different idea.'

Adele gave Michael a wistful smile.

'Don't people make things difficult for themselves? I seem to have spent most of today listening to people's problems. Tony and Jenny are adults who should be able to sort out their problems, you know.'

'But I really think they would be happy together. Isn't there any way we could give them a helping hand?'

'There is still a day before Tony leaves. If we see a chance to help them we'll take it.'

She stood up, brushing a few dead leaves from her skirt and as they took the downward path she looked at him mischievously.

'At least worrying about your sister's love life is better than having to worry whether she has been kidnapped or not.'

'There is that.' Michael sighed. 'But people seem to get into such weird situations when they fall in love! Thank heavens I haven't fallen for anyone!'

She gave him a sidelong glance. Was he deliberately making it clear that he saw her as a friend and nothing else?

'Let's get back. I feel like a nice long gin and tonic to start the evening.'

Michael didn't hear the coldness in her voice. He was frowning again.

'At least my parents' savings are safe. You know, I'd just like to know how that horrible little man and his friend with the motorbike got hold of Jenny's scarf. That was the only proof they could give that they were holding Jenny, and I fell for it.'

He halted abruptly.

'I haven't told Hassan that Jenny is safe! He's probably still searching Kas for that man! I should have thought of him before! I'll go and see him in the morning. Do you want to come?'

'I'd like to see him again,' she admitted.

Adele had been prepared to take Helen somewhere for a quiet dinner for two, but apparently working their way together through the shops of Kas had formed a bond between Helen and Mrs Brereton, and so she and Adele accompanied the Breretons that evening as they set out to have dinner. Tony, however, had sent a message that he had a lot to organise before he returned home. Both Michael and

Adele noted how downcast Jenny looked when she heard this.

They made their way along the seafront, and their path led them near the bus station where a bus that had made the two-hour journey from Dalaman airport had just arrived. Passengers were spilling off it. One man stood alone in the road, clutching a holdall and frowning. He stood out in the crowd, for he was dressed in a formal grey suit that was more suited to a London businessman than someone intent on enjoying the holiday atmosphere of Kas. Adele gave him a casual look, and then stared incredulously, as recognition dawned and she heard Helen's delighted cry.

'Roger!'

The man looked up and dropped his holdall as Helen ran towards him. His arms went round her eagerly and as everyone looked on with interest, they embraced each other passionately. Finally he released Helen.

'I love you!' he said forcefully. 'I was

going to wait at home till you got back from your holiday, but I was missing you too much. Anyway, after what you said I wasn't sure you would come back to me.'

The onlookers waited for Helen's reaction, and were delighted when she murmured incoherent denials of any such intention and then kissed her husband again. At this point, Roger Perry became aware of the spellbound audience and blushed fiercely. He looked round, saw Adele and gave her an embarrassed smile. After a quick exchange with his wife, he picked up his bag in one hand while Helen clung to his other arm and the two of them began to walk back in the direction of the hotel, the Breretons and Adele obviously forgotten.

Mrs Brereton turned to Adele, eager for information.

'That was Roger, Helen's husband,' Adele confirmed.

'I guessed it must be. But she gave me the impression that there was some trouble, that they were breaking up!'

'Fortunately, they seem to have got over their problems,' Michael observed dryly. 'Now, shall we go and find a table in the restaurant?'

Later, Adele thought how profoundly grateful she was that Roger had not arrived twenty-four hours earlier and discovered his wife in the act of trying to seduce Tony! Her practical mind did begin to wonder also about possible difficulties with accommodation now that Roger had appeared. However, there was no need to worry. Helen was just stuffing the last of her possessions into a bag when Adele reached the door of her room.

'It's all right,' she said happily. 'Roger and I have got a room on the next floor.'

'I am glad. Do I take it that you and Roger are reconciled?'

Helen nodded eagerly.

'Of course we are. I only flirted with Tony because I was so unhappy. As soon as a I saw Roger, I knew that I still loved him.'

Adele was too kind to remind her of some of her comments about Roger. Instead, she smiled and congratulated her friend, then closed the door behind her and collapsed gratefully on her bed. So at least one couple was happy!

It felt very pleasant to have the room to herself and a bathroom free of Helen's clutter. She could relax now. Jenny was safe, Helen was back with Roger, and surely Jenny and Tony could be brought together without too much trouble?

But when Adele and Michael were preparing to set off to see Hassan the following morning, they found that Tony intended to tag along with them.

'I've been to his shop. I'd like to have another look,' he said.

Michael looked at his friend sternly.

'You don't care about Hassan or his shop. You are just trying to avoid Jenny because you know you still owe her an apology. Well, if you are leaving tomorrow, you will have to say goodbye to her sometime. She's gone to spend the morning swimming and sunbathing while our parents are at the amphitheatre. Why don't you follow her?'

Tony looked panic-stricken.

'How can I, when I was so rude to her?'

'You can find out whether she'll forgive you or slap you,' Michael said ruthlessly. 'Come on, Adele. Whatever Tony is going to do, he isn't coming with us.'

They left Tony standing uncertainly in the road and walked off.

'Do you think he will go and see Jenny?' Adele murmured, resisting the impulse to look behind her.

'He's a fool if he doesn't,' Michael said briskly, 'in which case, he doesn't deserve my sister.'

When they reached Hassan's shop, they saw a figure in jeans and a white shirt brushing at some of the carpets, but when he turned round they saw that it was Hassan's assistant. He welcomed them in and offered them the traditional tea and then, to their surprise, he asked them if they knew where his employer was. He seemed very perturbed when they said they hadn't heard from him since Adele last called at the shop.

'He should have told me he was going away. I can look after the shop for a few days, I have done it before, but then he will have to be here to pay bills and answer letters,' the young man complained.

'When did you last see him?' Michael demanded.

'The day after you saw him. He was busy in the shop, went out for a short time, and just said goodbye as usual when we closed that evening. I opened the shop in the morning as I normally do, and waited for him, but he never came.'

'Have you tried to find out where he might be?'

'He has not been to the warehouse, because I telephoned them. No-one seems to have seen him.'

'But surely, when your employer

disappears without warning, you should contact the police or somebody?'

The assistant spread his hands.

'Tell the police then find he is with some girlfriend? Sometimes he has been away for a day because of that. He has parents in Istanbul but I do not want to worry them unnecessarily, so I thought I would wait till I saw you.'

Michael was frowning.

'Why did you think we might know?'

'Well, he did say that he had to tell you about Ali. He said you were trying to find him.'

Michael put down his cup very gently. It took a few minutes to extract all the information. Hassan had returned from his brief afternoon excursion, evidently pleased with himself. He told his assistant that he had tracked down a man called Ali, and that his friend Michael would be very pleased, though he did not tell the assistant why.

'Did he tell you the man's second name?' Michael asked urgently, but the assistant shook his head, obviously growing even more worried as he sensed Michael's concern.

'Should I telephone his parents? Should I tell the police?' he asked anxiously.

Michael looked undecided.

'I'm not sure. We don't want to cause trouble for him or upset his parents if we can avoid it. If only we knew more about this Ali!'

'His neighbours might be able to give you information about him,' the assistant ventured, and Michael stared at him.

'His neighbours? You know where Ali lives?'

'I know the road. Hassan did not tell me his full name or exactly where he lives, but he did tell me which street.'

Five minutes later, Michael and Adele left the shop. They had a sketch map showing the road where Ali lived, and the assistant had promised to call Michael's mobile if Hassan reappeared.

'What are we going to do now?' Adele asked anxiously.

'We're going to find out as much as we can about Ali, the fake kidnapper.'

Adele stopped, and he swung round impatiently.

'What's the matter?'

'I think this is getting beyond us,' Adele told him. 'These people were hoping to get a lot of money from you. If they discovered that Hassan was threatening their plans ... ' She gulped, her imagination full of horrifying pictures. 'They may have turned violent.'

'You mean they may have killed him?' he said bluntly.

She nodded.

'I think we should tell the police everything.'

'I've already had to tell the police that Jenny turned up safe and sound, and they weren't very happy when they found out that they had been wasting their time over a silly girl who'd had a quarrel with her boyfriend. Now do you want me to go back and tell them that I forgot to add that two men were trying to get money out of my family by pretending they had kidnapped her and my friend has vanished?'

She was silent. He had a point. It would be very awkward to have to tell the police that they had been concealing information from them, but Adele thought there was another reason why Michael did not want to go and see them. She remembered his frustration when Jenny was still missing and he had not been able to do anything about it except wait for news. Now his friend was missing and he had a chance to take action.

'I'm going to see if I can track down Ali,' Michael said. 'Are you coming with me or not?'

Curiosity made her nod, and without further discussion they made their way through the streets of Kas. The road was easy to find, but information about Ali was elusive. People they stopped and asked did not seem to know anyone of that name who lived in the street. The only person who did claim to identify him directed them to an address where a venerable man in his eighties admitted that he was called Ali but knew nothing about Hassan. They apologised for disturbing him and were about to retreat when he laid a hand on Michael's arm.

'There is another Ali,' he said thoughtfully. 'We don't really think of him as living here because he spends most of his time in Istanbul with his cousin, a waiter in one of the hotels there. If you go down between those two houses you will find where he lives when he is here.'

Adele and Michael thanked him profusely and followed the direction of his pointing finger.

'Presumably this cousin works at the hotel where Jenny stayed and he found the scarf or stole it. When I went there he would have learned from gossip in the hotel that she was missing and I was coming to Kas, so he dreamed up the false kidnapping,' Michael reasoned.

They made their way through the

narrow gap between two houses and found themselves facing a ramshackle, one-storey building that scarcely deserved the dignity of being described as a house. Its rough wooden shutters and plank door were firmly closed.

'It looks as if it was originally used for keeping animals. Anyway, it seems as if our friend was right. I don't think anybody is there now.'

Adele was half-disappointed and half-relieved. There was not going to be a confrontation with pseudo-kidnappers after all. But with a sinking heart she saw Michael was advancing on the building.

'We might as well have a look round,' he said.

8

The building was built into the hillside and it was clear that the only access was via the two small windows and door at the front. Michael rapped on the door and pushed fruitlessly at the shutters.

'We are wasting our time,' Adele said impatiently.

'Wait a minute,' he instructed her, bending down to look at the lock on the door. 'This doesn't look very strong.'

'Michael! You can't break in!'

'I'm just testing, and anyway nobody can see us here.'

His idea of testing involved applying more and more pressure to the door, and when it failed to yield, Michael took a pace backward and then hammered his heel into the lock with the full force of his body behind it. The door gave way and Michael almost tumbled into the building.

Michael pulled her into the building, then pushed the door shut.

'There are wires to the place, so there must be light,' he muttered.

A switch clicked under his impatient fingers and they found themselves looking at a squalid room which obviously functioned as living, eating and sleeping quarters. It was untidy, with dirty plates and glasses on the bare wooden table and it smelled of rotting food and unwashed sheets.

'Judging by the dust, nobody has been here for days,' Adele said.

'He may have left some indication of where he was going,' Michael said, rummaging through the litter, but in a few minutes he had to admit that there was nothing to help them find Ali.

'There's nothing here for us,' Michael announced resignedly.

Adele made for the door and he followed her, only to trip on a sheet trailing from the bed. He clutched at the table to save himself, and there was a crash as he knocked a large jug on the floor and then more noise as a chair tipped over.

'Quick! Let's get away in case any of the neighbours heard that!' Adele exclaimed, but Michael suddenly stopped and listened intently.

'There's a noise somewhere — somewhere in the house.'

As they stood in silence, a thudding sound could be heard faintly. It was difficult to tell where it came from.

'It's not under the house,' Michael murmured.

'It's from somewhere at the back.'

'But there's nothing there except a shower room.'

Michael braved the squalid shower room. A more careful examination found a narrow panel on the far side that proved to be not a cupboard but a door, bolted top and bottom. The thudding was coming from beyond the door, and now they could hear shouts as well.

'Stand back and get ready to run,' were Michael's instructions as he grasped a bolt.

The door swung open and a figure stumbled out from a pitch-black cave, threw a feeble blow at Michael, and then collapsed on the floor.

'It's Hassan!' Michael exclaimed.

Hassan was filthy, unshaven, and one side of his face was badly bruised. He sat up, blinked at the light, focussed on their two anxious faces, and managed a travesty of a smile.

'So what took you so long to find me?' he challenged, then passed out.

Adele hurriedly fetched a cup of water while Michael picked up his friend and supported him on a chair. Soon he regained consciousness and drank the water eagerly, and this time managed a rather lop-sided smile.

'I've been dreaming of that!' he said, handing the cup to Adele.

'What happened?' Michael questioned, but Hassan looked round and shuddered.

'Let's get away from here before I tell you anything. There's always a chance Ali and his friend may come back.'

With Adele and Michael supporting Hassan on each side, they managed to get him back to his shop. His assistant greeted him with delight, then took a second look and poured out a torrent of worried Turkish to which Hassan replied briefly.

'Take me upstairs to my flat,' he instructed Adele and Michael. 'I need a wash and some food!'

Michael helped his friend to the bathroom, turned on the shower, and then came to the immaculate little kitchen where Adele had managed to open a tin of soup and tip it in a saucepan.

'Hassan's covered in bruises, and feeling sore and very stiff,' he reported.

'Should we call a doctor?' Adele asked, but Michael shook his head.

'He'll recover in a few days, and a doctor might ask too many questions.'

He watched her stirring the soup and then started searching in the cupboards.

'What are you looking for?'

'Coffee. Hassan likes it strong and sweet.'

'Then ask the lad downstairs to make it, and tell him to make enough for the three of us.'

When Hassan appeared in the living-room, swathed in a white towelling robe, the coffee and soup were waiting for him together with some rather dry bread, and for a few minutes he devoted himself to the food greedily, finally looking up with a happy smile.

'I never realised how much I could miss coffee,' he sighed.

Michael leaned forward impatiently.

'Now, tell us what happened to you, and what you know about Ali.'

Hassan looked at them ruefully.

'What happened was that I was a fool. I asked around after you came to see me and it wasn't difficult to find someone who knew your man and where he lived. I was told that he'd lived in Kas for some years on and off, but he spent more time with his cousin in Istanbul. Everybody spoke of him as an unimpressive little man who scraped a living doing various odd jobs for people, so I didn't have the sense to take any elementary precautions, such as telling my assistant where I was going. I went to his house, tried the door and found it wasn't locked, so just like you, I decided to have a look round. I know most of those houses have a storage room dug out of the hillside and I thought Jenny might be held there.'

He looked embarrassed.

'Of course, Ali and another man came back while I was there, we had a fight, and then one of them hit me on the head with something hard. When I came round I was in the storeroom. At least they left me with a torch and some bread and water, not the style of living to which I am accustomed. Then the battery started to run low in the torch, so I had to turn it off and sit in the dark. I just sat, wondering what was going to happen to me.'

He struggled to sit upright, wincing slightly.

'I think the time for playing amateur

detectives is gone, Michael. We must go to the police and get them to help us rescue Jenny.'

'Rescue Jenny?' Michael said blankly, and then, as Hassan looked at him in surprise a tide of red rose in his cheeks. 'There's no need, Hassan. I was so eager to get you safely back here that I never thought to tell you. Jenny's safe at our hotel. She never was kidnapped.'

Hassan listened incredulously as the story of Jenny's reappearance was told. At the end he looked at them with confusion.

'But Ali told you they had Jenny. Why should they lock me up if they hadn't kidnapped her?'

'Because Ali and his cousin hoped to collect the ransom money from me before Jenny reappeared. They obviously saw a chance to make some easy money by bluffing, and nearly got away with it. They are just a pair of small-time crooks.'

'Small-time crooks who attacked me and imprisoned me?'

'Well, you were in Ali's house, and they must have known you are my friend. They could have killed you. Instead they just shut you away safely with some food and drink. I think they must have intended to release you when they had the money, or at least let us know where we could find you.'

'So everything has ended happily,' Adele told Hassan. 'Jenny is safe and you are free, and Ali and his cousin won't get any ransom money.'

Hassan looked at her sternly.

'You are forgetting one thing.'

They looked at him, puzzled.

'Revenge!' he exploded. 'I have been attacked, confined, humiliated. I want revenge!'

'You could tell the police that Ali and his cousin imprisoned you,' Adele began, and then paused. 'But you would have to say that you were in Ali's house, and then you would have to explain everything from the beginning, and they are not very happy about Jenny and her disappearing act anyway.

It might get very complicated.'

'I don't want to go to the police! I want to get my revenge personally!'

'Well, Ali isn't going to come back to Kas openly now his plan has fallen through, because Adele and I might see him.'

'But he doesn't know the plan has gone wrong!' Adele said excitedly. 'If he's been keeping away from Kas because he doesn't want us to see him, then he probably doesn't know Jenny is here!'

The two men looked at her for a long moment, and then Hassan's lips curled in a thoughtful smile.

'You are right, of course. There is every chance that the two of them will keep that appointment, expecting Michael, as a devoted brother, to bring them the ransom money in exchange for his dear little sister.'

He swung round to face Michael, his eyes gleaming.

'Instead, they will find two of us waiting for them, and not the money.'

Michael was smiling now, nodding agreement.

'It will be a pleasure.'

Hassan leaned back, looking satisfied.

'I shall look forward to it. And now, if you will excuse me, I shall go to bed for a very long sleep. In the morning I shall have a large breakfast and find out what has been happening to my shop while I have been unavoidably detained elsewhere.'

On the way back to the hotel, Adele turned on Michael angrily.

'You aren't really going to meet those men, are you?'

'Of course,' Michael said firmly.

'But there's no point! And they might be dangerous! Look what they did to Hassan.'

That was the wrong thing to say, she realised, as Michael looked at her coldly.

'You mean you don't think Hassan and I could cope with the two of them? I assure you, we can be dangerous as well. Ali and his cousin have caused both of us a lot of grief, remember.'

'Then go to the police! Going looking for a fight is so primitive.'

'And so satisfying,' Michael interrupted with finality.

'You're being stupid!'

'Thank you,' he said icily. 'But after all, it's nothing to do with you.'

The silence that followed lasted until they parted at the hotel.

Adele was furious with Michael and Hassan for planning to court danger deliberately, furious with Helen for virtually tricking her into a holiday that had been anything but the rest she desired, and furious with Jenny for being the cause of the whole complicated affair.

Now, Michael had made it painfully clear that she was no longer required as companion or helper, and Helen would be with Roger, so what was she supposed to do with the remaining days of her holiday? A faint memory stirred. Five minutes' search among her papers confirmed the dim memory of having booked an excursion for the next day to the hometown of Saint Nicholas, better known as Santa Claus. It was doubtful if Helen would remember or want to come, but at least it would get Adele away from all the Breretons. She set the alarm and managed to fall asleep.

Helen had not appeared when it was time for the excursion to leave, and Adele spent several hours admiring what was claimed to be the original church of Saint Nicholas and other sites which she would normally have found fascinating. On this occasion, however, instead of listening to the guide she frequently found herself brooding on what had happened since she came to Turkey, and wondering what would happen next. She got back in the late afternoon, tired and with a headache, and her temper was not improved when she saw Helen and Roger lounging in the hotel bar with cool drinks, looking as if they had spent a very pleasant day.

She joined them after a quick shower and showed more enthusiasm than she had actually felt when she described the places she had visited.

'It sounds quite interesting,' Helen conceded, 'but I wanted to be with Roger,' and she gazed at her husband adoringly.

Then Mr and Mrs Brereton appeared with Jenny. She looked for Michael, but was told that he was driving Tony to the airport. Adele had forgotten he was leaving that day, and regretted that she had not had an opportunity to say goodbye to him.

The whole group was planning to dine together, but Adele said that she was too tired after the excursion and wanted to go to bed early. As the others left the hotel, Jenny lingered long enough to snatch a quick word with her.

'I've got such a lot to tell you,' she whispered. 'It's about Tony and me!'

She was obviously bursting with news, and Adele promised to find an opportunity to talk to her the following day.

When she woke the next morning, her first thought was that this was the day Ali had appointed to meet Michael and receive the ransom money. She hoped that Hassan and Michael had come to their senses and decided not to go to the rendezvous. Let Ali and his cousin wait fruitlessly and wonder what had gone wrong with their scheme. Wouldn't their disappointment be vengeance enough?

Jenny wasn't present but Helen and Roger were waiting with smiling faces when she came down to breakfast, and insisted that she spend the day swimming and sunbathing with them. They generally made it clear that they had decided to share their happiness by being kind to poor, lonely Adele. In the face of such relentless cheerfulness she could have throttled both of them, but remembered other times when Helen had atoned for some previous bad behaviour by trying hard to help her friend when she needed it, and gave them credit for their good intentions.

Helen revealed why she thought Adele was in need of kindness when she asked if Adele had quarrelled with Michael.

'He was very quiet and gloomy yesterday after he heard you had gone out for the day and hadn't bothered to tell him about it.'

'I have decided that Michael Brereton and I have very little in common,' Adele told her, and refused to elaborate.

Adele came down ready for the evening before the others and decided that she would enjoy a short walk by herself. Telling the receptionist that she felt in need of a little exercise, she slipped out of the hotel and started walking along the coast road away from the town until eventually she found herself by the little rocky beach where Ali had hoped, possibly still hoped, that Michael would bring him a small fortune that night.

Adele was not quite sure why she had come there. She certainly wasn't going to wait to see if the sham kidnappers or Hassan and Michael appeared. She sat down to watch the sun sink into the sea and found herself thinking over the past few days. It had been an eventful holiday, but on the whole everything had turned out well for everybody — everybody, that is, except herself and possibly Michael. She shrugged. They had been thrown together by events and he had found her a useful confidante. That was all, wasn't it? He had made it painfully clear that he didn't feel the slightest bit romantic about her.

Adele stirred uneasily. She would find it difficult to forget him. Perhaps if they had met under different conditions, when he was not distracted first by his search for his sister and then by looking after his parents, things might have turned out differently.

The temperature had fallen now and she shivered as she looked round the little beach. She tried to imagine Michael and Hassan confronting the two men later that night, but it was difficult to imagine violence in that tranquil setting. Adele stood up. It was time to go back.

9

Adele began to walk slowly towards the hotel, her head bent. In a little over forty-eight hours, she would be back in England and she could forget the Breretons. She was so busy telling herself this that she did not see the man striding towards her until he greeted her.

'Adele!'

She jerked to a halt and found herself facing Michael.

'You idiot! I thought you would come to your senses after your macho showing-off! Are you planning to hide somewhere so you can ambush Ali and his cousin if they appear? What good do you think a fight with them will do? They'll probably end up beating you, and serve you right!'

Now anger reddened his face.

'Thank you for your confidence in

my fighting abilities!' he snapped. 'Actually, I was looking for you. The receptionist told me you had come this way, and I wanted to speak to you privately. In fact, I wanted to tell you once Hassan and I had calmed down we did decide that we would leave well alone and not try to confront Ali and his cousin. I was going to apologise for the way I spoke to you the other night, but I don't see why I should now.'

'Oh!' Adele managed to say. 'How was I to know that?'

'If you'd given me a chance to speak to you yesterday I could have told you. It still doesn't seem right that those two shouldn't suffer after all they have put us through, but slugging it out on the beach wouldn't do much good, and we did realise that. So you've guessed wrong about me yet again, Miss Pearson.'

Adele's chin took on a defiant tilt.

'Is it surprising? You always give me good cause!'

Michael sighed, and then put his

hands on her shoulders.

'You owe me an apology, and you know it!'

Then his grip tightened and he drew her close and kissed her. She felt herself begin to relax under his hands, and then abruptly he set her free.

'I didn't mean to do that! But I do mean to do this!' he said fiercely, and his arms went round her and he was kissing her again.

Later, much later, it seemed, they decided it was time to walk back to the hotel, but now they walked hand in hand.

'I wanted to get to know you the first time I saw you,' she murmured. 'I would have bought a carpet from you without a second thought.'

'I've wanted to kiss you since you tried to give me the money for that dinner, but I was looking for my silly sister and it never seemed to be the right time. Still, we seem to have ended up as friends, which isn't a bad beginning.'

She stopped walking.

'A beginning? Michael, I'm flying home tomorrow night!'

'So soon? I've lost track of the days! And I've told my parents I'll stay on with them for a few days. They can do with a holiday after worrying about Jenny, but they really need me to help them get about. But we will see each other in England, I promise you that!'

She smiled wryly.

'Good. I shall look forward to that. It's just a pity that we couldn't have a few peaceful days together here.'

'We'll have tonight, anyway,' he said firmly. 'This evening, we'll go some-where for a meal on our own. We'll make some excuse to the rest of them. You never did get another look at Hassan's carpets. I'll tell them I'm taking you to choose one, and I don't know how long that will take, so we'll get a meal somewhere when we're free.'

Adele eyed him suspiciously.

'You thought that excuse up very quickly.'

He had the grace to blush.

'All right. I was planning to ask you if you would like to go to Hassan's anyway, so that I could have an evening with you without all the family plus Helen and Roger. It's beginning to feel we're always with a party.'

'Actually, I've decided I would like one of Hassan's rugs as a souvenir, so long as they are not too expensive. After all, I would like something to remind me of Kas. But we're nearly back at the hotel, and I don't want to spend the evening feeling that they are all talking about us.'

So they strolled up to the hotel with careful nonchalance, to find Jenny sitting alone and looking rather sorry for herself.

'Helen and Roger have gone off on their own,' she complained. 'Apparently they see these few days as a second honeymoon, and that means a romantic dinner for two tonight rather than with the Breretons. Mum and Dad will be along soon.'

'I'll go and get them,' Michael told her. 'You and Adele can wait here.'

It was clear as soon as he had left that Jenny wanted to confide in Adele.

'I've been trying to have a word with you all day,' she said.

Adele, her thoughts still with Michael, gave her a vague smile, which Jenny promptly took as encouragement.

'You'll never believe what has happened! Tony loves me! He came down to the beach when you and Michael went to see Hassan, and he apologised for what he said to me. I told him I was sorry for all the trouble I'd caused, and that I never meant to do it. We talked for a bit and then suddenly he said that he loved me, and that was why he had been behaving so oddly!'

Suddenly her lip trembled and she seemed on the edge of tears.

'But now he's gone back to England! I told him he could change his flight but he insisted that he had to get back to work. Surely, if he really loved me he would have stayed here with me.'

'Work is important,' Adele reminded Jenny.

'As important as I am? When he says he loves me?'

Adele wanted to think of Michael, of what they would say to each other that evening, and her patience suddenly snapped.

'Jenny, Tony and your family dropped everything to come out here to search for you when they thought you needed help. I got caught up in looking for you, and so did Hassan, but that doesn't mean that the world revolves around you all the time. We have lives apart from you. I'm glad that you and Tony have discovered that you love each other, but if you behave like a spoiled child just because he won't ignore everything else for your sake, you could ruin everything. Tony wants a woman who will be his partner, not an immature young girl who can't understand the importance of his career.'

Jenny's mouth opened and then shut wordlessly, and before she could think of what to say, Michael and her parents arrived, and she stayed silent.

Michael had obviously been telling his parents what he planned.

'Jenny, I've called the Mermaid and booked a table for the three of you. They're expecting you in about half an hour.'

'Where are you two going?' his sister wailed. 'We need you with us!'

'I'm going to buy a carpet with Adele,' he replied calmly, 'and you do not need me to look after you while you have a meal in a restaurant.'

Michael and Adele slipped away quietly.

'You know, Tony was right when he said we'd spoiled Jenny,' Michael commented. 'I think Tony might get bored with her if she doesn't grow up.'

Adele thought of Jenny with a touch of sympathy. The girl was getting a lot of hard lessons very quickly.

'Don't worry. I think she may be learning fast. Where are we going?'

'To Hassan's, first of all. He was

recovering well when I last saw him, and I would actually like him to show you some small rugs.'

Dusk was falling as Adele and Michael approached Hassan's shop, which was the centre of considerable activity. People were clustered round a white vehicle which Adele recognised as an ambulance, and as she and Michael craned their heads to see what was happening, two men carried a stretcher out of the shop. On the stretcher was a figure dressed in jeans and a white shirt.

'Hassan!' Michael exclaimed, and then a second later saw the figure of his friend emerge from the shop and follow the medics as they loaded the stretcher into the ambulance, whose doors closed behind them.

The ambulance drove off, leaving Hassan gazing after it.

'Who is it? What happened?' Michael asked urgently when he managed to reach Hassan.

His friend shook his head sadly.

'Selim, my assistant. I sent him out to see if there were any tourists passing who would like to come into the shop. Suddenly I heard an engine, very fast, and then a scream, and when I came out, Selim was lying in the road. I think he is just badly bruised, but the hospital will check. I suppose it was somebody driving too fast.'

'Turks are not the best drivers in the world,' Michael commented, and Hassan nodded sourly, then made a visible effort to become the charming salesman again as he turned to Adele.

'I've decided I would like a small rug, a prayer mat, to take back to England with me,' she told him.

Within minutes, Hassan was producing carpet after carpet. One especially caught her attention. Its rich dark colours glowed.

'It is silk,' he told her proudly.

'That means I can't afford it,' she said sadly, and forced herself to turn to the other rugs.

Behind her, Hassan and Michael

were in urgent conversation.

'I think I'll take this one,' she decided, choosing a pleasant rug, predominantly red.

'You will take this one,' Hassan said firmly, picking up the silk rug.

'No,' she said reluctantly. 'I would love it, of course, but the price must be too high.'

'You are not buying it,' he told her. 'I am giving it to you as a gift.'

When she protested, he smiled and took her hand in his.

'You rescued me from that cellar. In fact, you may have saved my life. Let me show you my gratitude.'

'You've got to take it. Don't hurt his pride,' Michael murmured.

Hassan smiled, and told her that the rug would be wrapped and ready for her to collect in the morning, and seemed genuinely pleased when at last she said she would accept the rug with much gratitude.

Adele was blinking back tears when Michael finally led her away.

'I'm happy!' she said indignantly when he asked what was the matter. 'Nobody has ever given me anything so beautiful before!'

They dined in a small restaurant where the food was Turkish, as were most of the customers. They already knew the facts of each other's lives, and now was time to explore more deeply into feelings and hopes and plans.

At the end of the meal, they drifted slowly back to the hotel. They kissed goodnight before they entered the pool of light outside the hotel. Once inside, they separated and as Adele approached her room, she saw Jenny opening her bedroom door. The girl smiled tentatively at her.

'Was it a good evening?' Adele asked politely.

'Quite good,' Jenny replied, and then hesitated briefly before saying, 'I told my parents how Tony and I felt about each other.'

'And what did they say?'

'They said I was a very lucky girl.'

'So you have their blessing?'

'They are happy about Tony, but they obviously think I've let them down with the way I've behaved, and I've got to admit that I have been pretty stupid. What can I do to make it up to them?'

'Well, you were supposed to spend some time doing field work in Turkey, weren't you? Why not see if you can still do that? It will show that you are serious about your studies at least.'

'But that would mean I wouldn't see Tony for weeks!'

'Prove you can do what you set out to do, and then you'll have years to be happy with Tony.'

Jenny said goodnight thoughtfully, and Adele escaped to the privacy of her own room, free to think of the changes a day had brought.

Early the next morning, as they had agreed, Adele and Michael were swimming in the calm sea, content just to be with each other. Her plane did not leave till after midnight, so she could leave her packing till late afternoon. Helen would go with her, of course, and Roger had succeeded in getting a seat on the same flight.

Everybody else had gone off on various errands and at mid-morning coffee time Michael asked what she planned to do for the rest of the day.

'Well, I must buy some small presents for the people at work.'

'Why don't you do that before lunch, before it gets too hot? Meanwhile I'll go and collect your rug from Hassan.'

'That would be kind of you. Tell him I'll call in to say goodbye later.'

Adele showered quickly and changed into a light dress. The girl receptionist was on the phone as she passed her, but waved at Adele urgently when she saw her and held out the telephone.

'There is a call for you.'

Puzzled, Adele took the telephone.

'Hello? Adele Pearson speaking.'

She heard a man's voice, very agitated.

'Miss Pearson, you must come at once. Miss Brereton, she has had an accident.'

167

Adele's grip tightened on the receiver. 'Is she hurt badly? Where is she?'

The line crackled and the man's voice grew indistinct. All Adele could gather was that Jenny had been taken to a house on the headland that dominated the bay. The caller urged her to get a taxi and come at once, giving her the name of the spot the taxi should go to.

Gripping her bag, she hurried down the steps into the street. She looked around desperately, hoping to see a taxi. She saw one driving slowly towards the hotel and waved frantically, but when it stopped, Jenny and her parents got out, chatting happily and obviously in perfect health!

Her bewilderment must have shown, for they met her anxiously. What was the matter? She shook her head and indicated to the taxi driver that she had changed her mind.

'Nothing now. Someone thought you'd had an accident, Jenny. There must have been a muddle.'

She forced a smile.

'Well, there is no emergency, fortunately, so I'll go and do my shopping.'

But as soon as they were safely out of sight in the hotel, Adele grasped her bag and started to hurry in the direction of Hassan's shop. She was beginning to feel afraid.

10

Adele was looking for Michael as she neared the carpet shop, but instead she saw Hassan outside. For once there was no welcoming smile. Instead he was obviously furious.

'Vandalism! Sheer vandalism!' he said, pointing at a large carpet.

Looking at it, Adele saw that the complicated pattern was disfigured by pale splashes.

'Someone has thrown bleach or some other acid on it!' Hassan explained. 'It's completely ruined!'

'When did it happen?'

'It must have been done quite early, soon after I put the carpets out. There are never many people around at that time and it would only take seconds to attack it. Of course, I only noticed it when the bleach had got to work. But who would do such a thing, and why?'

Adele laid a hand on his arm nervously.

'I think I know. Can we go in the shop? I must talk to you.'

He gave her a sharp glance and then guided her inside. She sat down and he stood in front of her, waiting.

'Hassan, it was getting dark last night when Selim was knocked down. Perhaps it wasn't an accident. He was wearing a white shirt and jeans like you, so perhaps someone thought they were attacking you. Now that carpet has been spoiled, and it could be by the same person.'

'You mean I have an enemy who is trying to hurt me?'

'Not just you.'

Hurriedly she explained about the mysterious telephone call.

'If the Breretons hadn't appeared unexpectedly, I would now be somewhere on that headland, willing to go wherever someone wanted to take me, because I thought they would take me to Jenny.'

'So who do you think is responsible?' Hassan asked.

'How about Ali and his cousin? I was worried that you and Michael might try to revenge yourselves on them. But suppose they are trying to revenge themselves on you, on us? They were hoping to get a lot of money. If they came back and found out that Jenny had turned up here safely and that you had been freed, then they must have realised that all their scheming, the risks they had taken by attacking you, had been wasted. There would be no chance of getting the ransom and also the police might be looking for them. Perhaps they felt that vengeance would be some consolation.'

'It's possible,' he admitted. 'Ali would be too scared to try anything like that by himself, but from what I've been told, his cousin is vindictive and can be dangerous. He left Kas in the first place after he beat someone up in a bar. You may be right. They dare not risk staying in Kas for long if they have come back, but they may have decided to cause as much trouble as possible in the few hours they can spend here while they get ready to leave permanently.'

'We must tell Michael,' Adele said urgently, standing up and making for the door. 'He is in danger as well. In fact he will be their main target.'

'Michael left a short time before you arrived in order to take your rug back to the hotel. In fact it was after I said goodbye to him that I saw the carpet had been damaged. If they were watching the shop, they may have followed him! I'm coming with you.'

Hastily Hassan shut the shop door and shouted in Turkish to a man outside the next shop.

'My neighbours will keep an eye on things,' he explained to Adele.

The streets were busy now, as Hassan pointed out.

'Ali and his cousin wouldn't dare do anything to Michael when there are so many people about, and he'll be safe in the hotel.'

But when they asked the receptionist if Michael was in his room she shook her head.

'Mr Brereton came back for a short time, but then he went out again.'

Hassan and Adele looked at each other helplessly. Where should they start looking? The receptionist came to their aid.

'Mr Brereton had his camera. He said he was going to walk along the coast road and take some pictures.'

They thanked her quickly and set out along the road, but saw no-one until they reached the small beach where Michael and Adele had encountered Ali. Michael had obviously climbed down to the beach and walked to the water's edge to get a good view. To their horror, they could see that Ali and his cousin had found him there. Michael was trapped and stood with his back to the sea as the two of them advanced towards him. Ali might not be much of a threat but his cousin was a big, muscular brute.

Hassan ran towards the cliff, leaped down on to the beach, and raced towards the two attackers. As they heard the noise of his thudding footsteps they turned to see who it was, and in that instant, while they were distracted, Michael launched himself at them. It was a brief, messy and primitive fight. Adele hovered on the cliff top.

Hassan and Michael were fit, young and furious, and Ali was soon on the defensive, trying to protect himself from Hassan's blows. His cousin fought on till Michael tripped him and the big man fell into the sea with a terrific splash. He stood up, drenched, found himself facing two angry opponents alone, and dropped his hands by his side in surrender.

Hassan spoke to him roughly, then turned and consulted Michael before issuing what sounded like an ultimatum. Ali and his cousin shambled up the beach, heads hanging in dejection, and walked past Adele without giving her a glance. The cousin hauled his motorbike out from under a bush, and he and Ali climbed on it. The engine spluttered, and then the two of them were riding away at top speed, away from Kas.

Michael, his arm round Hassan's shoulder, was shaking hands with his rescuer, and when Adele went down to join them she saw that although they were the winners they had suffered in the fight. Michael's cheek was bruised, his shirt was torn, and Hassan had a cut over his eye.

'You're letting them go?' Adele demanded.

Somehow she had imagined the two men would be triumphantly dragged off to the police station, but Michael nodded, then sat down on a rock and hung his head, drawing in deep breaths.

'That is the only fight I've ever been in since I left school,' he said finally, 'and as far as I am concerned it can be the last!'

Hassan, crouched beside him, nodded his agreement.

'What happens now?' Adele asked them.

'Nothing,' Michael said. 'The reasons we didn't want to get involved with the police still apply. What we have done is tell the two of them that we are going to make sure that everyone in Kas knows what they have done. They won't dare come back to the town because life would be made very uncomfortable for them. Anybody who threatens tourists also threatens the livelihood of a lot of people in Kas. They've also had to abandon the house and any possessions they had. That will be punishment enough. It's all over, Adele. You've got a few hours of holiday left, so let's enjoy it. I think I'll go back for a shower and some clean clothes.'

'I'll do the same, and then I'd better re-open my shop,' Hassan said.

In the end, Adele waited for Michael at the hotel and then they went together to Hassan's shop where he welcomed them, clean and elegant once more. To their surprise, Selim was there also, his head bandaged and moving gingerly as though bruises were hurting him.

Hassan insisted on taking them to lunch at a small place where everybody seemed to be his friend. While he chatted to the people at the nearby tables, Michael and Adele sat quietly.

'What time do you leave today, Adele?' Hassan enquired, momentarily finding time to speak to his guests.

'The coach picks us up at eight this evening,' she told him.

Adele wondered if he was thinking the same as she was. It was all very well to say that, of course they would see each other when they returned to England, but once back home it might be difficult to keep that promise. Michael lived in Cambridge, Adele in London. They would be busy with their different careers. Oh, they would probably see each other a few times, but at increasing intervals, until finally they would find keeping in touch took too much effort.

She gave a little sigh and smiled at the two men.

'I really must go and buy those souvenirs,' she told them.

'Why don't you go now while Michael and I tell everybody here about Ali and his crooked cousin?' Hassan suggested. 'Come back to my shop afterwards and I will give you both a last cup of coffee.'

But when Adele arrived at the shop an hour later, there was no sign of Michael.

'He remembered something he had to do,' Hassan said vaguely. 'Now, let Selim prepare our coffee.'

Adele dutifully made small talk while they sipped the coffee, but her thoughts were drifting away towards Michael. Had he decided that it would be better to say goodbye now? Was his absence a hint that she need not expect to see much of him in England? She looked up to see Hassan regarding her sympathetically.

'You are sad to be going home?'

'Yes. Turkey is beautiful, and I do

179

lead a rather dull life in England.'

'You will come back to Turkey, I am sure.'

'Perhaps,' she said sadly.

Soon afterwards she said goodbye to Hassan, promising to return to Kas if it were possible, and went back to the hotel to pack. At half past seven she was sitting in the reception area with her luggage by her side, ready to board the coach. Helen and Roger were there with their suitcases as well, holding hands and smiling at each other from time to time. It was obvious that their reconciliation was complete. Mr and Mrs Brereton were also there with Jenny, eager to thank Adele for her help. Jenny found an opportunity to confide to Adele that Tony had telephoned her and she had told him that she intended to stay on in Turkey for fieldwork. He had approved, though he had assured her that he would miss her.

Only Michael was missing.

Punctually, at eight o'clock, the coach arrived and Adele, Roger and

Helen boarded it. Adele went last, reluctant to leave, looking round to see if Michael was going to appear at the last minute. She could not believe that he would let her go without saying goodbye, but as the coach set off on the long road to the airport there was still no sign of him.

Adele gazed out of the coach window, restraining angry tears. She had spent what was supposed to be a restful holiday advising and helping others, listening to their problems and trying to help them find solutions. Well, now things were going to be different. She knew that more than once she had not been promoted when a suitable vacancy had appeared because her boss found her so useful where she was, so the first thing she would do would be to look for a new job in some firm where she would be properly appreciated.

Then she would find somewhere else to live. Her landlady claimed she treated Adele as if she were her daughter, and this was true if being a daughter meant being handy when there were things to be done about the house. Adele knew that her unhappy childhood had left her reluctant to assert herself or make trouble, but from now on she would stand up for herself and do what she wanted. She would work hard and prosper.

The time at the airport dragged. She just wanted to leave Turkey behind her and was the first one on her feet when it was announced that it was time to board the plane. There was an empty seat beside her and she placed her handbag on it.

The last few stragglers were boarding the plane and the air hostesses had already started to check that all passengers had fastened their seatbelts when Adele's bag was lifted, dropped into her lap, and someone sat down in the empty seat. She turned and found herself staring at Michael! He looked back, unsmiling.

'You didn't come to say goodbye,' she heard herself saying.

'And I suppose that once again you jumped to the wrong conclusion about me and thought I didn't want to.'

Before she could reply, the air stewardesses were going through the ritual of taking everyone through the safety drill. As soon as that was finished, Michael was speaking again.

'I decided yesterday that I couldn't bear to be parted from you so soon, that I wanted to come back to England with you. I persuaded Jenny that she could look after our parents for a few days as well as I could, then I went to the travel agent's, only to be told that I had left it too late to book a seat on this flight. There didn't seem to be anything I could do. Then this afternoon I told Hassan. He has friends in every business in Kas, so he telephoned and then sent me off to see someone in an anonymous little office in Kas. He told me I could possibly get a seat if I went to the agency's head office in the next town, so off I went in a taxi.'

Once again came the familiar gesture

of running his hand through his hair.

'There were a lot of negotiations on the telephone while I just sat there wondering what was going to happen. Finally, when I'd given up hope, I was suddenly given a ticket! I dashed back in the taxi and got to the hotel five minutes after your coach had left, so I called Hassan, threw a few things in a bag, kissed my family goodbye, and then Hassan arrived in his car and drove me to the airport.'

He paused.

'That was definitely my most frightening experience in a car ever. But here I am. Please tell me that you are glad to see me, because all the time Hassan was hurtling round dangerous corners I had this fear that perhaps you had decided that you didn't want to see me again after all, that you were glad to slip away without having to say goodbye. Jenny and my parents said you didn't ask them where I was.'

Adele was smiling, with tears in her eyes.

'I'm glad you are here, near me,' she said softly, then leaned across and kissed him full on the lips, not caring who saw her. Michael gave a great sigh of relief and seized her hand in a grip that hurt.

'I shall be near you for as long as you want me to be, and I hope that will be for the rest of our lives,' he said fervently.

They had had a bad beginning, but the future was now looking bright . . .

The End

We do hope that you have enjoyed reading this large print book.

Did you know that all of our titles are available for purchase?

We publish a wide range of high quality large print books including:
Romances, Mysteries, Classics
General Fiction
Non Fiction and Westerns

Special interest titles available in large print are:
The Little Oxford Dictionary
Music Book, Song Book
Hymn Book, Service Book

Also available from us courtesy of Oxford University Press:
Young Readers' Dictionary
(large print edition)
Young Readers' Thesaurus
(large print edition)

For further information or a free brochure, please contact us at:
Ulverscroft Large Print Books Ltd.,
The Green, Bradgate Road, Anstey,
Leicester, LE7 7FU, England.
Tel: (00 44) **0116 236 4325**
Fax: (00 44) **0116 234 0205**